ALFIE BLOOM

Also by Gabrielle Kent:

*Alfie Bloom and the Secrets
of Hexbridge Castle*

ALFIE BLOOM

and the
Talisman
Thief

Gabrielle Kent

SCHOLASTIC

Scholastic Children's Books
An imprint of Scholastic Ltd
Euston House, 24 Eversholt Street
London, NW1 1DB, UK
Registered office: Westfield Road, Southam, Warwickshire, CV47 0RA
SCHOLASTIC and associated logos are trademarks and/or
registered trademarks of Scholastic Inc.

First published in the UK by Scholastic Ltd, 2016

Text copyright © Gabrielle Kent, 2016
The right of Gabrielle Kent to be identified as the author
of this work has been asserted by her.

ISBN 978 1407 15580 7

A CIP catalogue record for this book
is available from the British Library.

Printed by CPI Group (UK) Ltd, Croydon, CR0 4YY

Papers used by Scholastic Children's Books are made
from wood grown in sustainable forests.

1 3 5 7 9 10 8 6 4 2

This is a work of fiction. Names, characters, places, incidents and
dialogues are products of the author's imagination or are used
fictitiously. Any resemblance to actual people, living or
dead, events or locales is entirely coincidental.

www.scholastic.co.uk

For my family

1

Raiders from the Oak

Alfie rolled on to his back and smiled up at the stars as the wind whipped through his hair and flapped his pyjamas. He patted the fur beneath him – flying bearskin was the only way to travel.

"You're quiet tonight," said a deep voice by his ear. "Everything OK?"

"Just enjoying the peace, Artan." Alfie reached back and scratched the bear's head. The whole rug rippled beneath him as Artan growled with pleasure.

The moonlight glinted off Lake Archelon, highlighting the silhouette of Hexbridge Castle sitting high atop one of the hills overlooking the village. Alfie still couldn't believe he lived there. His dad was fast asleep inside and so was his best friend Amy Siu, who was staying for the Easter holidays while her gran recovered from a bad bout of flu. His cousins Madeleine and Robin had left a few hours ago after spending the whole weekend at the castle.

Alfie loved having so many people around, especially after his former life in a gloomy basement flat with only his dad and his cat, Galileo, for company. Inheriting a magnificent castle from Orin Hopcraft, the last of the great druids, had changed his life completely, but he still enjoyed his own company sometimes. Where better to be alone than in the clouds?

It seemed like years since Christmas, when his head teachers, Murkle and Snitch, had turned into a dragon and tried to eat him. The ancient magic Orin had hidden inside Alfie had saved the day by stripping away their magic, but the feeling of power it had given him as he used it was almost as terrifying as the dragon. He shivered despite the warm night; he still had nightmares about it sometimes.

Tonight's dream had been the worst yet. He had turned into a dragon and eaten his family. It felt so real that he could have sworn his arms were still green and scaly when he woke up. He'd taken to the skies before going back to sleep. A peaceful flight usually cleared his mind, but this time the nightmare was hard to shake. He touched the talisman that always hung around his neck. Feeling it there, keeping the magic inside him hidden and controlled, helped him to feel safe.

"OK, take us home, Artan."

"Homeward-bound," rumbled the bear. "Hold on tight!"

Alfie buried his fingers into Artan's thick fur as the bear turned in a big swooping arc over Wyrmwald House school before soaring back towards the castle. Alfie was enjoying school life since Murkle and Snitch had been arrested. He hoped they'd be locked up for a long time somewhere very far away. His favourite teacher, Miss Reynard, had taken the role of headmistress. Alfie was pleased about that. She seemed the least likely person to turn into a ferocious dragon.

They glided over Archelon Lake towards the gentle roar of the river that flowed around the castle before cascading over the cliff behind it as twin waterfalls. As the bear sailed over the castle walls, the oak tree in the cobbled half of the courtyard caught Alfie's eye. It was lit with a blue light that flickered out almost as soon as he noticed it. Was he imagining things? He clamped his hand over Artan's muzzle and pointed down. Artan nodded and quietly floated over to land behind the stone battlements.

Popping his head up to peer through one of the gaps in the stonework, Alfie could just make out a shadowy figure moving around near the tree. The drawbridge was still up, so how had someone managed to get in? The figure moved out from under the tree and headed towards the castle doors. Alfie leapt to his feet, but just as he opened his mouth to yell down at the intruder, he recognized the figure as Ashford, the butler. He dropped back down behind the stonework, not wanting to explain what he was doing out in the middle of the night. He watched the butler tuck something small into his pocket before heading into the castle. Alfie wondered what he was doing up so late.

Waiting until Ashford had closed the door, Alfie gave Artan a pat and they swept up to his open bedroom window. He still hadn't told any of the adults about the bear. He was half afraid his dad would want to run experiments to figure out how he could talk and fly. Only Amy, Madeleine and

Robin knew about him, and they were under strict instructions to keep their lips zipped or else lose their flying privileges.

The bear glided silently through the sleeping castle. Alfie hopped off outside the castle library and Artan floated back to his cosy little room in the southern tower. Alfie was still wide awake after his nightmare. He grabbed a few of his favourite comics from the library to read in bed, hoping they would help to replace the dragon in his dreams.

Passing the staircase, Alfie heard an unfamiliar voice echoing up from the ground floor. He froze and listened. It was melodic yet harsh. Every word carried menace.

"You were a fool to return. Did you think we would forget what you stole from us?"

Slowly, Alfie lay down on the carpet and peered through the banisters into the hall below. There were four people down there in the dark. Three of them were very tall and wore long tunics with some form of leather waistcoat. They were holding on to the arms of the shortest figure, who was struggling to free himself from them.

"Tell us where it is."

The sharp-faced owner of the voice stood almost nose-to-nose with their captive, who answered defiantly, "The one place you'll never be able to take it from. Muninn and Bone's vaults."

The second voice Alfie knew well. Ashford. The castle was being burgled and the robbers were threatening their butler! Alfie didn't know what to do. He could wake his dad and Amy, but two twelve-year-olds, a butler and a skinny inventor would be no match for the fierce-looking men in the hall.

There was a grunt from Ashford as one of the men drove a fist into his ribs. Looking around frantically, Alfie spotted a large sword held by a suit of armour. He considered grabbing it and charging down the stairs but doubted he'd even be able to lift it high enough to threaten the thieves.

"You will take us there."

"No one can travel there without one of their coaches," replied Ashford.

"Then call one."

The man was holding a knife to Ashford's neck. Alfie's instincts took over. He leapt to his feet and threw his full weight against the suit of armour, sending the whole thing crashing down the stairs.

"Hey, you! What are you doing? Get out of here!" he yelled at the top of his voice as the armour crashed and banged its way down the stairs. He picked up one of the shoulder pieces and clashed it against the wall, hoping that if he made enough noise the men would think there was a whole army upstairs.

"Alfie, duck!" shouted Ashford.

Alfie dropped to the floor, and not a second too soon. Three arrows thudded into the tapestry behind him in quick succession.

"What's going on?" shouted Alfie's dad, dashing out of his bedroom at the same time as Amy emerged from hers in tartan pyjamas, brandishing her baseball bat.

"What is it, Al? Are you OK?"

Alfie crouched behind the stone balustrade, making himself as small as possible as the two of them raced down the corridor towards him. "Stay where you are!" he shouted as he kicked out at another suit of armour, sending it toppling downstairs after the first. "They're firing arrows!"

"Who, Alfie? Who's down there?" called his dad over the clanging and clattering of metal.

"I don't know," mouthed Alfie. He pulled his arms in tight just as another arrow chipped the stone near his elbow.

The last piece of armour crashed down into the hall below. Alfie risked a peek. A fight had broken out. Ashford had wrestled himself free and was spinning furiously, aiming punches and kicks at the intruders with pinpoint accuracy. *Where had he learnt to fight like that?* Alfie wondered. One of the men was on the floor near the bottom of the stairs; the other two were circling warily, waiting for a chance to attack.

"What do we do?" whispered Amy, wriggling across the floor towards Alfie on her elbows.

Alfie was wondering that himself. His dad seemed to have a plan, and had grabbed a shield and spear from the walls as he crawled over to join them.

"Get to one of the bedrooms and lock the door until you hear my voice," he hissed over the yells and crashing sounds from below.

Alfie stared at his dad. He had never seen him look so fierce and determined. "No way! You can't go down there alone. I'm not leaving you."

"You don't have a choice. Get to your room. I'll help Ashford." Before Alfie could argue there was a yell from Amy. She had leapt to her feet and was shouting down over the banisters.

"Ashford! Look out!"

Another figure had appeared in the doorway: a woman. She was tall, with a coldness to her angular features, and she stood with a bow raised to her shoulder. Ashford hadn't seen her; his face was turned up towards Amy. Alfie joined Amy in screaming and pointing towards the door. Ashford turned and two of the men leapt at him, trying to pin him down. He fought his way out of their grip, but it was too late. The second his eyes met those of the woman at the door, she released her arrow. It tore through his clothes and thudded into his shoulder, the sheer force of it knocking him to the ground.

"No!" Alfie and Amy screamed as one. Alfie ripped the spear from his dad's hand and hurtled down the stairs, screaming at the top of his lungs, his dad and Amy following close behind.

A sack was pulled over Ashford's head as his attackers dragged him towards the doorway where the woman with the bow stood, her pale face lit up with cruel delight.

"Stop! Leave him alone!" Alfie yelled, hurling the spear in fury. It clattered uselessly to the ground behind the intruders as they disappeared through the door. He leapt down the last few steps and charged across the hallway.

"Alfie, wait!" called his dad, but then he let out a cry of pain. Alfie looked back to see him tumbling over the armour that littered the stairs. Amy stopped to pull him to his feet as Alfie sprinted out into the courtyard, leaving them behind,

The oak was lit up again with the weird blue light. This time Alfie could see that it was coming from a gaping hole in the tree's trunk – it was some kind of portal. Ashford's captors stepped through into the light, dragging Ashford with them.

"Stop!" Alfie shouted as he ran. He reached the tree just in time to see Ashford's feet disappearing through the portal. With barely a thought, Alfie thrust his arms into the light. It felt cool and rippled like water around his arms as he grabbed hold of what felt like a leather waistcoat. He planted his foot against the tree trunk and pulled as hard as he could, staggering back as a figure emerged. It was the woman who had shot Ashford. She was smiling, her beautiful green eyes glittering with malice as she grabbed his wrists in a vice-like grip and twisted until he let go of her clothing. Alfie cried out in pain, struggling to free himself.

"Get off him!" screamed Amy, racing towards them. Alfie's dad followed, limping badly. Just as Alfie's wrists felt like they were about to snap, the woman released her grip with a cry of rage. Amy had batted one of her baseballs through the air to smash into her cheek. A purple bruise blossomed instantly on the woman's luminous white skin. She snarled something at Alfie in a language he didn't understand. Amy threw herself on to the woman like a wildcat but was swept aside with an effortless blow that hurled her across the courtyard. The woman turned and stepped back into the tree.

"Alfie, stop!" called his dad as Alfie lunged towards the portal.

He could barely see anything through the light that suddenly surrounded him. He tried to take a step forwards, but his dad's hands grabbed at the back of his pyjamas and he felt himself being dragged back out of the tree.

"No!" he screamed, straining to move forwards, the portal crackling around his ears as his legs were pulled back into the night air. "We've got to stop them taking Ashford!"

He could hear his dad and Amy screaming his name as he held on to the sides of the portal and struggled against their grip, willing all the strength he could muster into his arms. Straining to pull himself forwards, his fingers appeared to twist into claws, and scales ran up his arms, just like in his dream. Was the portal doing this to him?

As he tried to blink away the image, a figure

materialized through the blinding light. It was the sharp-faced man who had threatened Ashford. His cold eyes were emotionless as he stared down at Alfie. His foot snapped out to kick Alfie in the chest, sending him flying back through the portal, where he landed in a heap on top of his dad and Amy. Struggling to catch his breath, Alfie watched the portal shrink back into a long blue line before its light winked out completely.

Staggering to his feet, he frantically pounded his fists on the bark, but the portal was gone. And so was Ashford.

2

The Stolen Lens

Alfie gazed at the threadbare arm of the sofa he had slumped on to – each loose thread jarringly clear. They had gathered in the Abernathy Room, in which Alfie's dad had recreated the living room of their flat in Abernathy Terrace. Their old furniture felt comfortingly familiar now.

It hurt each time Alfie took a breath but the shock of Ashford being torn from them was more painful than his bruised chest and wrists. Amy was sitting next to him and his dad was holding an ice pack to her eye, which had already started to swell.

"Are you OK, Dad?" Alfie asked, breaking the

numb silence they had fallen into since the portal closed.

"I'll live." His dad left the ice pack with Amy and limped painfully over to his armchair. "But what have I told you about leaving things on the stairs?" Alfie couldn't even muster a smile at his dad's weak attempt to lighten the mood.

"Are you going to call the police?" asked Amy.

"That's what I'm trying to figure out. What would we tell them?"

Alfie knew his dad was right. Caspian Bone, their strange solicitor, had worked some kind of magic over the whole village – no one remembered that a dragon had nearly destroyed the town before Christmas. Inspector Wainwright would think they were nuts if they told him that Ashford had been dragged through a magic portal in the oak tree.

The old brass telephone in the hall began to ring. Alfie jumped to his feet, glad of an excuse to get out of the room, which seemed to be closing in around him. Crossing the silver shafts of moonlight cast down into the entrance hall through the landing windows, he picked up the receiver. A sweet voice spoke with a serious tone.

"Alfie, it's Emily Fortune, senior administrator

at Muninn and Bone. Our ravens have told us what has happened. Don't try to follow Ashford. Close the doors and keep out of the courtyard until the phone rings three times. Caspian Bone is sending a carriage for you."

Emily's voice made Alfie feel calmer. Caspian might be odd but Alfie was sure he would know just what to do in a situation like this.

Thanking Emily, Alfie put down the receiver and noticed his cat, Galileo, prowling the area where Ashford had been attacked. He was sniffing the ground, hackles raised as he emitted a low growl.

"It's OK, boy." Alfie reached down to stroke him, but Galileo slipped out from under his fingers, crouching low to the ground as he darted outside, following a scent to the courtyard.

"Leo! Get back here." Galileo was sniffing around the tree. Alfie called again but the cat paid no attention to him. After pretending to close the large castle door several times Alfie gave up and closed it completely. He guessed Galileo would be able to look after himself.

"Caspian is sending a carriage," said Alfie as he rejoined his dad and Amy. "We've got to stay inside until the phone rings."

"In case they come back?" asked Amy. "Do you think they will?"

"I don't know. They wanted something from Ashford. I think they've taken him to get it for them."

"What if he refuses?"

Alfie didn't reply. He didn't want to think about the danger Ashford was in.

Twenty minutes later the phone rang three times. "That's the signal. Come on." Alfie hooked his arm around his dad and helped him limp to the door.

Amy's jaw actually dropped as she saw a polished black coach sitting in the courtyard. Alfie recognized it as the very one that had taken him and his dad to Muninn and Bone's offices nearly a year ago, where he had first learnt he was to inherit Hexbridge Castle. Six midnight-black horses steamed in the moonlight as they stamped on the cobbles.

Johannes the driver nodded to them. The coach door clicked open. Two short, stocky, bearded men in leather overalls and stout boots jumped out and grabbed a heavy black bag from the back of the coach. They dragged it towards the oak and then circled the tree, tapping it and scratching their beards while making tutting noises.

Leaving the two men to examine the tree, Alfie climbed into the velvet darkness of the carriage, followed by his dad and Amy. He felt out of place in the elegant interior and wished he had changed out of his pyjamas first.

"You are hurt."

They jumped as a voice sounded from the shadows. The oil lamps in the carriage dramatically flared to life to reveal Caspian Bone sitting opposite them. "Your injuries will be tended to at our offices."

"Caspian!" cried Alfie, his chest hurting as he shouted out with relief to see the solicitor. "Someone took Ashford. They dragged him into that portal thing in the oak tree. We've got to get him back!"

"They shot him with an arrow," burst out Amy. "They were really tall and strong; we couldn't stop them."

"I didn't know whether to call the police," said Alfie's dad. "I mean, what would we say? What *could* we say?"

Caspian listened to their wild ranting in impassive silence, and then rapped the wall behind him with a black-and-silver cane. The coach began to move. "Your police cannot be of help. I will deal with this matter alone." Over Caspian's clipped tones Alfie could hear the horses clatter over the drawbridge, their hooves pounding the ground as they galloped down the hill. As they reached full speed the coach tilted back as though the horses had leapt into the air and were galloping into the sky. He noticed Amy straining to see through the black glass windows.

"Are we fly—" began Amy.

"Not important," interrupted Caspian. He twitched his head back to Alfie, who noticed Amy raise an eyebrow at being cut off so sharply. "The talisman – is it safe?"

Alfie pulled it from his pyjamas and showed the solicitor.

"Good. They still think it is at our offices. We have arranged for the oak to be bound with iron so that the elves cannot return through that portal while we negotiate Ashford's return."

"Wait . . . *elves*?" asked Alfie. "Those people were elves? Are you serious?"

"Do I ever joke?"

Alfie thought that would be too much to hope for.

Amy's other eyebrow joined the first as Caspian casually confirmed the existence of a supposedly mythical race. "What did they want from Ashford?" she asked.

"I suppose it serves no purpose to keep the information from you now that they have found him again."

Alfie was even more surprised that Caspian was about to give him some answers than he was about the revelation that elves exist.

"The lens in the talisman," continued the solicitor. "They wanted it back."

"My talisman?" asked Alfie, automatically reaching for the golden disc hanging from his neck. He ran his thumb over the spiralling runes that encircled the purple lens fixed into its centre.

"Alfie's talisman belonged to the elves?" asked his dad.

"Not the talisman itself – the lens that sits within it. It is made from a rare gemstone, one of a kind. It can focus and control other powers and energies. The lens was designed to focus the powers of a crown the Queen of the elves had been developing for centuries. She intended to use it to expand her realm, enslaving other tribes and races. An elf close to her warned us of their plans and my partner, Mr Muninn, enlisted Ashford – a talented thief who was duty-bound to us – to take it from them. Ashford agreed when he heard that the druid Orin Hopcraft needed a lens such as this to create a talisman – the talisman that controls the magic he hid within you, Alfie. When Ashford returned, we sent the lens back to Orin. Much as I detest thieves, I will acknowledge that this theft saved many lives, as well as protecting yours. But it appears that the elves never gave up hope of retrieving the lens. How they found Ashford, I do not know."

"Ashford stole it ... for *me*?" said Alfie, holding the talisman tightly in his fist. "He didn't even know me!" The only thing that had been making him feel a bit better was the fact that the kidnapping wasn't related to his inheritance, and now Caspian was telling him that it was. He could hardly breathe.

"Believe me when I tell you that it was as much in his own interest as yours."

"Are you saying that you sent a wanted thief to work for us?" asked Alfie's dad incredulously.

"Yes," said Caspian coldly. "But a thief who has pledged his loyalty to your family. You may trust him completely."

It wasn't like Caspian to praise Ashford. Alfie

had always suspected there was some unspoken history or rivalry between the two.

"Why is the talisman so important to them? Enough to half kill him for!"

"Emily Fortune will discuss the minutiae with you when we arrive. I must attempt to open negotiations with the Queen. We have sent a coach for her. Ashford has told her that we hold the talisman here, but if they break him they will find a way to return to the castle and get it."

"Break him? They're going to torture him?" cried Alfie. "Then you can't waste time talking to this Queen; you have to find him and stop them! If they want the talisman I'll give it to them. Just get him back!"

The oil lamps flickered, sending shadows dancing around the carriage as Caspian's expression darkened. Amy snapped her eyes away from the window and they all shrank back a little in their seats as the solicitor seemed to tower over them without even moving.

"I do not *have to* do anything – except observe proper customs and protocol. We do not charge into another people's land and jeopardize peace with brash demands. Do not presume that you have any say in this. Giving up the talisman would risk the lives of many for just one man." The lights stopped flickering and the darkness fled as Caspian leaned back into his seat.

Alfie's stomach was churning. Ashford could be getting tortured while they spoke, and there was nothing he could do about it. He glanced at Amy. For the whole journey she had remained as cool as if she was in an ordinary car, but by the way that she was sitting so stiffly he knew she didn't like the way Caspian spoke to them at all. Alfie was used to the solicitor's coldness by now, but Amy never let anyone get away with trying to intimidate her. She looked Caspian up and down.

"Who do you think you are?" she asked. Alfie exchanged a nervous glance with his dad.

"I beg your pardon?"

"You heard me. *You* might not have an ounce of compassion, but *our* friend has been hurt and kidnapped and all you can do is talk down your big nose and bully Alfie into shutting up."

Caspian glared and the lights started to flicker again.

"Don't start that nonsense." Amy got to her feet and pointed at him. "You're not half as intimidating as you think you are. You're Alfie's solicitor. It's *your job* to help him and answer his questions. So stop being so . . . so obtuse!"

The carriage was silent as Amy and Caspian seemed to be locked in some kind of staring competition. Alfie held his breath. Caspian broke the silence first.

"Obtuse?"

"Yeah. It's a word. Look it up!"

"I *know* what it means," said Caspian. Alfie wasn't sure, but he thought he might have seen the slightest trace of a smile flicker across Caspian's lips. He spoke again in a very slightly softer tone. "I'm afraid I am not one to offer false hope and reassurance. The most you can do is hope that there is something, other than the talisman, that she is willing to accept in exchange." Alfie and his dad stared at Amy in a mixture of amazement and admiration, unable to believe that she had faced down the haughty solicitor.

At that moment the coach bounced and shuddered. The horses dropped from a gallop to a canter before slowing to a stop. Alfie wondered if he would ever be allowed to travel up top with Johannes to see their journey. He didn't think it was likely – everything about Muninn and Bone's operations seemed extremely secretive.

The doors popped open and Alfie leapt out into the huge coach house, glad to be away from the silence that had descended on the carriage. Johannes jumped down to tend to the horses as Caspian swept ahead, leading them through the door to the entrance hall. Alfie could tell that Amy was dying to stop and investigate the array of coaches as they hurried after Caspian.

"Emily will join you shortly," said the solicitor as he strode across the grand reception to stand on the round brass crest that served as a lift to the upper floors. The brass cylinder that formed the walls of the lift descended from the ceiling. "I must prepare to meet the Queen and begin our negotiation." The cylinder clanked down around him. There was a hiss of steam and a whooshing noise that lasted nearly a minute before the cylinder retracted back into the ceiling, leaving them alone in the entrance hall.

3

The Greatest Thief Who Ever Lived

"OK, I didn't want to say anything in front of that pompous git," exploded Amy, "but that coach was awesome, and the journey here? *Crazy!* This place is so weird! Where are we?"

"A long way from home," said a gentle voice behind them. A small woman with huge green eyes had entered the hall. She was smiling at Amy's ill-timed outburst, but didn't seem quite her usual bubbly self.

"Emily!" shouted Alfie, rushing to greet Caspian's administrator. He realized too late that he wasn't sure whether to hug her or shake hands, and ended up delivering an awkward combination of the two.

"Smooth," Amy whispered out of the corner of her mouth as she came over to introduce herself.

"Oh, your poor face!" said Emily. Amy's left eye was swollen and her cheek was turning a nasty shade of purple. "Come on. Let's get you all fixed up."

Alfie had hoped they would be taking the odd lift Caspian had used, but the route Emily took them on was even more interesting. He was amazed to see behind the scenes of Munnin and Bone's strange offices as they followed Emily down corridors high enough for a giant. His dad hobbled along, his arms around Alfie and Emily's shoulders as they passed small meeting rooms, grand halls and an elegant ballroom. In one room a very old little man on a tall rickety ladder on wheels skated between towering filing cabinets. A multi-level room nearby was full of chattering people tapping away on old-fashioned typewriters.

Emily opened a huge door and they went outside briefly to cross a large internal courtyard. In the centre was an enormous tree with hundreds of ravens nesting in its twisting branches. The birds cawed loudly down at them as they walked past. Alfie wished he had more eyes to take everything in as Emily led them into another wing of the building. He wondered just how big the whole place was.

Each row of tall arched windows that lined the various corridors seemed to look out on to a different scene. Through the first Alfie could see a night sky filled with swirling coloured galaxies. The second looked out on to a desert city roofed with golden domes that shone in the sun. Through the third was a vast lake fed by dozens of roaring waterfalls. Amy ran ahead, calling out what she could see.

"How is this possible?" asked Alfie's dad as he hobbled along. "Are we even in the same building we entered?"

"Our offices are multidimensional," said Emily. "A kind of hub between worlds. That's what makes them so secure." Alfie didn't even have time to be amazed at the revelation as she hurried them down yet another corridor. This one was lined with pillars carved with intertwining Norse patterns. Its windows looked out over what Alfie could only describe as a modern interpretation of a huge Viking city. *Where on earth are we?* he wondered.

"Phew, sorry about the long trek, but here we are," said Emily. "This wing is part of Mr Muninn's world. He's not around, as usual. Oops, forget I said that, shouldn't speak ill of the boss, but really, I wish he'd arrange cover for when he heads off on his long expeditions – I'm sure it's all very important, but it does rather leave us in the lurch when he ups and leaves and it's not like I can even broach the subject with him – I remember when I first started here and all I did was ask where. . ."

"Does she always talk like this?" Amy whispered in Alfie's ear as Emily recounted the whole conversation in a single breath. He nodded.

". . . can you believe that?" Emily finished. "On my first day too. Needless to say, I never mentioned paper clips ever again. Ooh, he's a stern one is Mr Muninn." Alfie had never met Caspian's business partner but couldn't imagine anyone being as prickly as Caspian Bone.

Emily stopped and opened a burnished copper door. Alfie blinked against the brightness as they followed her through. They were in a large round room constructed of white marble with a stained-glass-domed roof. A large tree grew from the centre of the room and up through the centre of the dome, where its canopy gently shaded the room from the sun. Tiny colourful birds the size of bees darted between the flowers that covered the vines climbing up around the tree. Emily motioned them to three reclined throne-like chairs.

As Alfie settled into one of the seats, three tall women dressed in long robes silently entered the room. All three had white blonde hair coiled up in plaits. They took up positions by the chairs and laid out jars and bandages, then set to work rubbing salves and ointments on to bruises with long, slender fingers. As the doctor tending to Alfie smoothed a thick green ointment over his bruised chest, he could feel the ache ebbing away and his breathing become less painful.

"That's amazing," said Alfie, as the bruising already seemed less vivid. "What is that stuff?" His dad and Amy seemed to be dozing off in their chairs as the doctors worked their magic.

"Only the best treatment for our clients," smiled Emily. As Alfie's doctor finished bandaging his chest and rubbing strong scented oil on to his sprained wrists, Emily held out her hand. "Come walk with me." Alfie clambered out of the chair and thanked the woman who had been treating him. She gave a graceful bow of her head in return.

"They have taken a vow of silence to enhance their powers of healing," said Emily as Alfie followed her from the room, leaving his dad and

Amy sleeping. "As the others are asleep, I thought we could talk." She led Alfie to a balcony that jutted out from the corridor. They sat on a stone bench looking out over the strange city. It was a few minutes before she spoke again.

"Was Ashford badly hurt?" Emily's hands were clenched tightly together in her lap as she gazed straight ahead. "When our ravens brought the message that the castle had been invaded, they said that he had been shot – with an arrow."

"It went into his left shoulder." Alfie flinched as he remembered the sound the arrow had made as it struck bone. He felt sick. "It was quite high up. I think – I think he'll be OK if they treat the wound."

Emily bowed her head and flicked at an imaginary spot of dirt on her dress. She seemed to be holding back tears as she spoke about Ashford. Alfie realized that she had been putting on a brave face since they arrived. He looked at her restless fingers and wondered if she thought of Ashford as more than just a friend.

"Treating him will be the last thing on their minds," she said in a quiet voice. "They want the lens and won't let him rest until they have it. I don't know how they found him."

Alfie remembered the blue light he had seen flickering around the tree when he returned from his flight on Artan. "I think he had been using the portal. The one that opened in the oak. I saw him near it, not long before they came through."

Emily's face froze. "I don't believe it. He went back into their realm? Why would he take such a stupid risk? You are very lucky that they didn't realize he had led them right to your talisman." She sighed. "Ashford has ... unusual skills, as I'm sure you have realized. Unfortunately, he is rash and impulsive. He made poor choices earlier in his life, using his gifts in a manner I am sure you would never dream of."

"Caspian told us he was a thief."

"The greatest that ever lived." Emily seemed to catch herself smiling and quickly adopted a disapproving expression. "Of course that's nothing to be proud of. His biggest mistake was trying to break into one of our vaults."

"He tried to break in here? What was he trying to steal?" asked Alfie.

"Nothing in particular – he did it for the challenge. It was amazing that he even managed to find a way here. Caspian wanted to see him imprisoned, but Mr Muninn thought he could be useful. The choice of prison or working for the firm wasn't much of a decision for Ashford. He has retrieved many stolen items for our clients."

"So *that's* why Caspian doesn't seem to like him!" said Alfie as everything began to drop into place. "And Ashford doesn't like Caspian because he was forced into working for him?"

"And because he caught him. The world's greatest thief, caught in the act. I can tell you, the atmosphere between those two was stormy at best when he was working here. Things certainly calmed down when he was sent to look after you."

"He didn't seem too pleased when he first moved in."

"At first, but he could hardly let Caspian know he ended up quite happy about it." Alfie wanted to ask more but she looked on the verge of tears again. She took a long breath then stood up. "Come on – Amy and your father will be awake by now."

A plate of colourful fruits and jellies was sitting on Alfie's chair when they returned. Amy and his dad were already tucking into theirs.

"Best doctors ever!" said Amy. The swelling around her eye had gone right down and even under the thick layer of green ointment he could see that it was less bruised. His dad was wriggling his bandaged foot around as though he'd only just discovered he had ankles.

Alfie was so exhausted he barely took notice of the strange views from the windows as they followed Emily back to the coach house. As she turned the handle of the door to the entrance hall she froze and quietly closed the door again.

"What is it?" Alfie's dad whispered. Raised voices were coming from the hall. Emily pointed to two spyholes in the door. Alfie and Amy stood on their tiptoes to peer through. Caspian was talking to someone Alfie couldn't quite see. The solicitor was dressed more strangely than usual. Instead of his Victorian-style suit, he wore a black tunic embellished with dark gems, long boots and a high-collared black cloak with delicate silver embroidery. A silver circlet rested on his raven black hair.

"I am grateful that you called us here to negotiate," said a woman's voice. "But I am disappointed that you refuse to hand back what is rightfully mine. Especially while we hold one of your own. Tell me," she stepped towards Caspian, "what is his life worth to you?"

Alfie could see her in full now. She was tall – as tall as Caspian – and she wore a long sky-blue dress that seemed to billow around her even though no wind was blowing. On her head was a crown made of delicate strands of gold twisted around shining gems.

"The Queen," whispered Emily. "She's acting much more quickly than I thought."

"*That's* the Queen?" Alfie burst out as he caught a glimpse of her face. "She's the one that shot Ashford!"

Emily said nothing, but Alfie felt a storm in her silence.

"We do not respond to threats," said Caspian coolly.

"Maybe not. But now that we are here, what is to stop us from taking it?"

Alfie held back a yell as the elves she had brought with her surrounded Caspian. He recognized three of them as Ashford's attackers. "They're going to hurt Caspian!"

"No," said Emily. "They're not. Now come on, they don't know that you have the lens. We can't risk them seeing you here."

Alfie and Amy remained glued to the spyholes as the elves closed in menacingly on Caspian. Looking nonplussed, he snapped his fingers. The suits of armour around the walls creaked to life and stepped down from their stands. "I don't believe it!" said Amy as the empty suits marched towards the elves and grabbed their wrists. The screams were ear-piercing.

"Iron! You would dare to use iron against us?" screamed the Queen as her retinue struggled uselessly against the armour.

"Shall we start again – with a more civil discussion?" said Caspian. The suits of armour released the elves and marched back to their positions against the wall.

"Come on!" said Emily grabbing the back of their pyjamas and pulling them away from the spyholes. "We need to get you home, now!" She led them through a different door and back into the coach house. Johannes was waiting atop the coach, and another carriage stood next to his. It was green with incredibly ornate silverwork trailing around the doors and roof. A driver that could have been Johannes's twin brother was tending to the six pure white horses that pulled it. Alfie realized that it must have brought the elves from their realm. He remembered what Emily had said about the offices being multi-dimensional and suddenly the huge variety of strange carriages in the coachhouse began to make sense to him.

"Quick, I've locked the door from reception, but you need to get out of here," said Emily, hurrying them into Johannes' coach. Alfie grabbed her arm before she closed the door.

"Emily, I know they don't like each other, but Caspian *will* try his hardest to get Ashford back, won't he?"

Emily grasped his hand reassuringly. "He never does anything less, Alfie. The oak portal will be sealed when you return. Do not, however impatient you might feel, attempt to go through it."

Alfie felt his dad grip his shoulders. "He won't." It was as much a command as a statement.

4

The Black Mirror

"Oi, sleepyhead!" *Thud-thud-thud.*

Alfie was wrenched awake by the sound of his cousin Madeleine hammering on his door and yelling through the keyhole. He could hear her brother Robin telling her off.

"Keep it down, Maddie. You're the most annoying alarm clock ever!"

Alfie wished that she had a snooze button as he rolled out of his huge four-poster bed and opened the door for the twins.

"Sorry, I tried to stop her barging up here," Robin apologized as Madeleine bounced into the room. Alfie rubbed the sleep from his bleary eyes.

"Your dad went food shopping," said Madeleine, poking through the comics on Alfie's bedside table. "He gave us some money to go for lunch with you and Amy. You know it's after one o'clock? Is she still in bed too?"

"Maddie, come back!" called Robin as his sister dashed off to wake Amy. He threw his arms up. "I swear she gets more annoying every day. Meet you in the courtyard when you're ready," he called back as he hurried after her.

Alfie dug out a pair of jeans and a T-shirt and tried to remember where he had kicked his shoes. He'd never get used to such a huge bedroom. By the time he had showered and dressed, Amy and the twins were already lounging on the grass in the courtyard's garden. He was very glad to see that Amy's black eye was almost unnoticeable now. He loved the castle, but the gifts he had received from Orin, especially the ancient creation magic the druid had hidden inside him, seemed to keep bringing danger to people close to him.

"What's up with the tree?" asked Madeleine. Alfie had almost forgotten about the strange men that Caspian had brought with him to the castle last night, but it appeared that they had been hard at work. Three iron bands encircled the oak tree, which Alfie guessed were to prevent the elves from opening the portal from the other side again. On each band was an indentation that, before even looking, Alfie knew the talisman would fit into. The talisman was already a key for many things that Orin wanted him to be the only person to open, such as the druid's study and the great seal under the castle. It seemed he was now the guardian of the portal too. This was another lock he would never open.

Alfie and Amy filled the twins in on what had happened during the night. They were too shocked by Ashford's kidnapping to dwell on the revelation that he was a time-travelling thief too.

"So that's *all* Caspian is doing to get him back?" cried Madeleine. "Talking? There must be something *we* can do." She leapt to her feet and began examining the bands around the tree. "Your talisman will open these, won't it? We could go after him. Me and Robin could bring our bows. We'll rescue him ourselves!"

"Sit down, Madeleine. You're not helping," said Robin wearily. "Even if we could figure out how to open the portal ourselves, what are we going to do? Go up against a pack of armed elves? You're not going to shoot anyone and they'd know that."

Alfie felt grateful to Robin as Madeleine sat down, finally silent. He knew charging after Ashford could only end in disaster but wished there was *something* he could do.

"What's Leo up to?" asked Amy, breaking the grim silence. Galileo was stealthily creeping across the grass nearby. Crouching low with ears flat to his head, he began to wiggle his bottom.

"He's going to pounce," said Alfie, recognizing the cat's hunting mode. Galileo suddenly shot forwards, leaping through the air to land in the middle of the herb patch. A large mouse shot out of the parsley, squeaking loudly. The cat darted after it as it scampered through the grass to disappear into a hole in the castle stonework. Galileo settled down in front of the hole. Alfie knew he'd be there for hours. He had seen the cat wait patiently for days when he was hunting. Watching Galileo waiting for his meal made Alfie realize just how hungry he was himself.

"Come on. Let's go for lunch."

Gertie Entwhistle in the village bakery was delighted to see them, and Alfie began to feel better after one of her freshly baked steak pies.

"I'd have thought that butler of yours would be

horrified at you eating anywhere but the castle," said Gertie as they paid for their lunch and bought bags of orange tongue-twizzlers and sherbet fizz-bombs from her little sweet shop at the front of the bakery.

"He's on holiday," said Alfie, thinking quickly. He didn't want news of the attack getting around the village and telling Gertie would be like putting an announcement in the local paper.

"A holiday?" said Gertie in mock surprise. "I wish I could remember what those felt like. I could do with a butler around here. I just can't keep up with business these days."

Alfie's dad was back with the shopping when they returned to the castle. He seemed to be trying overly hard to be jolly as they helped him unpack and stock the cupboards. It was the longest Alfie had seen him in the kitchen since they had moved to the castle, and it was clear he didn't have a clue where Ashford kept everything. Alfie could tell that Dad was still very uneasy. His eyes twitched to the window at every sound from the courtyard.

"I'm making lasagne tonight," he called after them as they headed back outside. "Be in the Great Hall for six. I don't want to have to wander all over this place looking for you."

Alfie groaned as memories of his dad's bizarre cooking came flooding back.

In the courtyard Galileo was crouched on the cobbles beneath the oak with something between his paws.

"What have you got there, boy?" said Alfie, creeping towards the cat. With a quick flick of his paw Galileo sent the mouse he had been stalking sailing through the air and leapt up to catch it again.

"Bad cat!" cried Robin. Galileo paid no attention, letting the creature run a little way before trapping it with his paws again.

"He's just doing what cats do," said Madeleine. "It's in his nature."

"He's tormenting it!" said Robin, who could never bear to see an animal hurt.

Alfie crept towards the cat. Galileo growled as he closed in, picking up the mouse in his jaws and springing to his feet. Alfie leapt forwards just in time to grab him around his furry waist. "Quick, get the mouse!" he shouted, as Galileo writhed in his hands, scratching at his arms. Robin gently eased the cat's jaws open, releasing the mouse into Amy's waiting hands.

"Poor little fella," said Amy, stroking the top of

the mouse's head as she carried it into the castle. Galileo followed, trying to claw his way up her jeans to reach the trembling creature. Alfie pulled him off her.

"What's wrong with you?" He deposited the cat in the kitchen next to his food bowl. "Anyone would think we were starving you!" He shut the door, leaving the cat to yowl his frustration at his lost prize.

"The mouse is OK," said Robin. "But we should keep an eye on him for a while before we let him go."

"There's an old birdcage in Artan's room," said Alfie. "Come on. We can put him in there."

The cage proved to be very suitable. It was nice and big, and the bars were close enough together to stop the mouse slipping out between them. They even found some straw to line it with. Artan floated over to see what they were doing as they placed the mouse inside with some sunflower seeds and a jam-jar lid filled with water.

"What type of mouse is that?" he asked.

"A common field mouse, I think," said Alfie.

Artan took a long hard sniff. "Smells funny."

"That's because Leo slobbered all over him," said Amy.

"Do you even have a sense of smell?" asked Alfie.

"That's right," rumbled Artan. "Mock the poor old hollowed-out bear. I'll have you know you couldn't pick a better nose than mine. Go on, give it a try."

"Urgh. Get away!" Alfie pushed the bear's cold nose away as it nudged his cheek.

"I will if you give me an in-*scent*-ive. Get it?" He did a little flip in the air as he cracked up laughing at his own puns.

The bear's jolly mood changed completely when Alfie recounted the attack of the night before. He became more and more agitated, swooshing around the room knocking masks and paintings off the wall in his clumsy rage.

"They came in here – to our *home* – and harmed one of our own? We should fly straight into their lands and give them a taste of fear!"

"Calm down," said Alfie, grasping the bear's paw and pulling him down. "You sound like Maddie. We're not going after them."

"Well, we should at least be prepared in case they come back," he growled.

"He's got a point," said Robin. "I know the portal is sealed, but we should be ready to protect ourselves – just in case. Think. You saw them at Caspian's offices. Is there anything you remember?"

Alfie thought hard and remembered how the elves had screamed in pain when the armour in Caspian's offices had grabbed their wrists. "Iron! It burns them or something."

"Of course!" said Amy. "That must be why Caspian had those little blokes ring the tree with iron."

"Robin, do you remember Granny's stories?" said Madeleine suddenly. "When we were little she told us she always keeps a cat in the house and an iron poker by the door. . ."

". . .In case the Fair Folk come calling," finished Robin, his eyes wide. "Do you think she was talking about elves? She couldn't really know something about them, could she?"

"Let's ask her tomorrow," said Alfie.

"Hey, look at this." Amy had been investigating the harpsichord and had found something. "I was wondering why some of the keys wouldn't work. This was hidden under the lid." She handed Alfie a curved black mirror in a round copper frame. It was about the size of a large saucer.

"I was wondering where Orin left that," grinned Artan. "Give it a go."

Alfie stared into the mirror, and a distorted reflection with a huge nose stared back at him.

"It's not a very good mirror," said Madeleine, polishing the surface with her sleeve. They took turns to look into it until Alfie's stomach broke the silence with a loud grumble.

"All right, calm down. It wasn't that funny!" he said as the others fell about laughing. "Let's go and see if Dad needs a hand in the kitchen."

"Alfie, the mirror!" cried Robin. Alfie looked at the curved disc in his hands and nearly dropped it in astonishment. In the glossy surface he could see a room with a little figure running frantically backwards and forwards.

"Let me look," said Madeleine, pulling at the mirror. The second it left Alfie's hands the image disappeared.

"Look what you did!" snapped Robin. "Why do you have to be so grabby?" He handed the mirror back to Alfie. "See if you can do it again."

Alfie stared down at it. "I don't know how it works. I just said 'let's go and see if Dad needs a hand in the kitchen—'" The mirror flickered to life again. "It's Dad!" he cried. They all watched as Alfie's dad soaked a tea towel in water before running back to throw it over a flaming pan.

"What is this thing?" Alfie asked Artan, who was enjoying watching their puzzlement.

"Orin's scrying glass. It was always handy for seeing who was at the door. Just tell it the room you want to see – it works for anywhere within the castle's walls, even the courtyard and gardens."

"Try another room," said Madeleine eagerly.

"OK, how about my bedroom?" The surface flickered and reflected a fisheye view of Alfie's room.

"Nice boxers, Al," laughed Amy.

Alfie went bright red and mentally kicked himself for leaving yesterday's underwear on his bedroom floor. "The Great Hall, the Great Hall!" he shouted quickly.

They spent half an hour viewing all of the rooms that they knew of in the castle, even making up names of rooms to see if they existed.

Alfie took the scrying glass and the caged mouse to his bedroom before they went down to dinner. The mouse sat quietly in the cage, front paws wrapped around the bars.

"It's like it's watching us," said Robin.

Alfie's dad met them on the stairs, his face red and sweaty and his hair sticking up more than usual. "Dinner is served!" he panted. "I've set out the table in the courtyard. Thought I'd let the castle ... er ... air out for a while."

Alfie was very glad that they were eating outside as a fog of burnt cheese seemed to be creeping into every corner of the castle. They trooped into the courtyard garden where plates and cutlery had been set out on the stone picnic table. He wondered if another reason they were eating out here was to keep an eye on the oak tree. He could understand his dad being worried. The fact that their home had been invaded in the middle of the night was terrifying. His dad seemed to be avoiding mention of Ashford.

"Ace lasagne, Mr B!" said Amy as she tucked in. Alfie was sure she was just being polite, but his dad seemed to swell with the praise.

The layers of sauce and cheese in the lasagne were separated with slices of toast. Alfie realized that his dad must have forgotten to buy pasta sheets. He sometimes wondered if his dad deliberately forgot ingredients to turn the preparation of a meal into one of his experiments.

"How's Lizzie?" Alfie's dad asked Amy as they ate. Alfie knew that Amy's gran loved working in her tea rooms and rarely took a holiday, so it must have been a very nasty illness to slow her down.

"Getting over the infection," said Amy. "But she asked if I could stay on until the end of the holidays. She said she has some stuff to sort out at the tea rooms."

"That's fine with me, but we'd understand if you'd prefer to stay on the farm with the twins after last night."

"Yeah!" said Madeleine immediately. "You could share my room."

"Cheers, Mads, but nothing could put me off staying in a castle," said Amy quickly.

"Leave those, Dad, we'll do them," said Alfie as his dad began to clear away the plates.

"Thanks, Alfie. I'm going to bed before I fall asleep right here. As it's the holidays you can stay up for another couple of hours, but make sure you use the security switch, and promise me none of you will go out into the courtyard."

"We promise," said Alfie.

"What's the security switch?" asked Amy after Alfie's dad had gone off to bed.

"Muninn and Bone had it fitted after Murkle and Snitch nearly tore the Great Hall apart before Christmas." Alfie led the way to a brass switch on the wall near the main castle doors. "Flick it."

Amy flicked the switch and a strange chorus of

clinking chains, sliding bolts and hissing pistons rang through the castle as the front doors bolted shut and iron grates rattled down in front of the stained-glass windows. The chandeliers and torches on the walls flared to life in the sudden darkness.

"Cool!" said Amy. "I can't see any elves getting past that."

"Yeah," said Alfie. "I just wish we'd used it last night."

"Don't beat yourself up, Al," said Amy. "Caspian's an arrogant jerk, but I bet he'll get Ashford back."

Alfie wished he shared her confidence. His fingernails dug into his palms as he thought about how much worse things could have been the night before. If only he'd used the security switch when he got back with Artan, Ashford would still be with them.

5

The Change Magic

Alfie woke abruptly from yet another nightmare about turning into a dragon. Something was brushing his face. He sat up quickly, dislodging Galileo from his chest, and patted himself down to check that his body was still human. The cat's tail was swishing from side to side as he watched the mouse in its cage on Alfie's desk.

"Wha-issit?" said Robin blearily from his inflatable mattress on the floor. Madeleine and Amy were sharing a room too. There were enough bedrooms for everyone several times over, but none of them felt like being alone after what had happened to Ashford.

"It's just Galileo," said Alfie, getting up and grabbing the cat. "He's obsessed with that mouse. I'm going to put him out."

"OK," said Robin, checking his watch. With the shutters down it was impossible to get an idea of the time. "It's seven o'clock. We might as well open up the shutters and let the mouse go. It looks fine now."

Alfie looked into the cage. The mouse was running in circles, squeaking agitatedly. It stopped as he approached and stood on its back legs to look up at him. It did look as though Galileo hadn't done any damage. He put the wriggling cat down on the floor, where it prowled around his ankles, looking hopefully up at the cage.

"Not for you!" said Alfie, wagging his finger. He picked up the cage. If he released the mouse in the courtyard and kept Galileo shut up for the day it would have time to get back to wherever it belonged.

Galileo let out a hopeful yowl as Alfie carefully carried the cage across the room. "No, you're staying in here," he said, nudging the cat back with his foot as he opened the door. "Robin, would you catch him?"

"OK," yawned Robin. "Here, fella." Galileo

hissed as Robin tried to grab him and clawed his way up Alfie's leg to swat at the cage.

"Ow!" cried Alfie, holding the cage out of the cat's reach. "Robin, get him off me!"

"I'm trying!" said Robin. Alfie felt the cat's claws rake his leg as Robin pulled the spitting creature off him. What had got into him?

Between the two of them, they managed to shut Galileo in the bedroom, and then they took the cage downstairs. The sunlight that flooded the dark entrance hall as Alfie flicked the security switch made him blink painfully. Several of Caspian's ravens were patrolling the castle walls, so Alfie released the mouse into the long grass across the drawbridge. The ravens watched it hungrily but stayed at their posts as it scurried away down the hill.

For breakfast, Alfie's dad reheated the remainder of the soggy lasagne, and prepared prunes, bran flakes and custard to follow.

"Tuck in. Got to keep yourselves regular!" he announced. Alfie nearly choked on a prune stone in his embarrassment.

The phone rang as they were washing the dishes. Alfie rushed to answer it. A slightly flustered-sounding Emily Fortune was on the other end.

"Alfie!" she exclaimed. "Is Ashford there?"

"What do you mean?" asked Alfie. "How could he be here?"

"We received a message this morning. They released him last night." She sounded a little concerned. "I thought he'd be there by now, but I suppose it depends on the gateway they used to send him back."

"Caspian did it? Ashford's free? I don't have to give up the talisman?" Alfie could hardly believe it.

"They said that they didn't want to break the peace between our worlds," said Emily.

"That meeting with Caspian must have scared the Queen into giving Ashford back," said Alfie, thinking of the iron knights. He wondered what other resources Caspian had up his sleeve.

"Maybe. I just never would have thought she'd be so . . . so reasonable."

"This is great news though, isn't it?" said Alfie, wondering why Emily wasn't dancing around the room when he was tempted to do so himself.

"Yes. Yes, I'm sure it is," said Emily, finally allowing herself to let out a little laugh. "It's the best news. He's coming home!"

Alfie let out a whoop of joy that made everyone rush out from the kitchen.

"They let Ashford go!" he told them. Amy and the twins hugged each other and such a look of relief ran over Alfie's dad's face, revealing just how worried he had really been.

"Alfie, would you mind if I pay you a visit?" asked Emily. "I'd like to be there when Ashford gets back."

"Of course," said Alfie, putting his hand over his free ear to block out the questions the others were shouting as he strained to hear what Emily was saying. "OK, see you this afternoon."

The castle and everyone in it seemed much more cheerful in the light of Ashford's release. Madeleine had gone back to the farm to help Granny with the sheep shearing, but made Alfie promise to call as soon as Ashford was home. Robin had been talking excitedly to Alfie's dad over breakfast about an idea he had for some sort of security device, should the elves ever return. The two of them disappeared into the workshop, where Alfie's dad had recently set up a small forge, to explore the idea.

Amy had promised her gran that she wouldn't leave her maths homework to the last minute, and went up to her room after lunch to catch up with it. Alfie had plenty of his own homework left to do but killed time batting Amy's baseball around the courtyard garden as he waited for Emily to arrive.

At around two o'clock he heard a car coming up the hill. He had been keeping an eye on the skies for a flying coach so was surprised when a white vintage sports car drove over the drawbridge. The roof was down and Emily waved at him as she pulled into the courtyard.

"Alfie!" she got out of the car and kissed him on both cheeks before untying her headscarf and shaking her long, dark hair free.

"You can drive?" said Alfie, feeling silly for asking even as he said it.

"We don't use the coaches during the day if we can help it," laughed Emily. "Besides, this is my day off." She held out her elbow to him. "Shall we?"

"Er, OK." Alfie hooked his arm through hers and she practically skipped into the castle alongside him. He found himself being dragged along behind as she twirled from room to room.

"It's been so long since I was last here," she smiled, whirling around the Great Hall. "You must show me everything you have found so far!"

Alfie took Emily on a whirlwind tour of the castle, taking in the kitchens, bedrooms, cellars, battlements and a secret passage from one of the bedrooms to a huge linen closet. As they squeezed out from between the piles of neatly ironed sheets, it suddenly struck Alfie that the castle didn't have a washing machine and he had never seen Ashford doing any ironing. Come to think of it, no one ever vacuumed or dusted either. It was just another remarkable mystery of Hexbridge Castle.

Emily raced up the steps of the southern tower as soon as Alfie opened the hidden door. He was getting tired trying to keep up with her.

"So, this is the great Artan," she said, as they visited the room where the bear lived. Artan floated into an upright position and delivered a deep bow.

"M'lady."

"I've heard tales of your heroics during your time with Orin," said Emily. "It's an honour to meet you at last, old man. I believe you and Alfie have become great friends?"

"I couldn't *bear* to be without him," said Artan.

Alfie rolled his eyes as Emily laughed at the joke. "We try not to encourage him," he whispered.

"Have you found the entrance to the eastern tower yet?" Emily asked later as they headed down to the kitchens. "I know Orin kept some of his greatest treasures there."

Alfie hadn't, but immediately put it to the top of his list of things to do during the holiday. He made a pot of tea and they drank it sitting in armchairs in front of the fireplace in the library. He told Emily about the strange dreams he had been getting where his arms turned scaly and green. He hadn't known who to talk to about it, but just telling Emily made him feel better.

"I thought I was dreaming it the first time, but I saw it clearly while I was trying to pull myself through the portal. I don't know what it was."

"I think I do," said Emily. She laid her hand gently on his arm, which made Alfie think he wasn't going to like what he was about to hear. "During your battle with Murkle and Snitch the magic Orin hid inside you took their power away. They couldn't change back into a dragon because your magic fed on theirs. It's a part of you now."

Archie felt sick. "But they were evil! You're saying their magic is inside me, trying to turn me into a dragon?"

"It's not trying to do anything," said Emily. "No magic is evil, or good. It just *is*. This is a change magic, but because it was only ever used by your headmistresses to change between dragon and human form, that is all it knows. A change magic could be very useful if you mastered it."

"I don't want it."

"Are you sure? Many would love to have that ability."

The idea of being able to change form was tempting. Alfie thought of everything he could do with it: become an actual fly on the wall to listen in on any conversation, impersonate anyone he wanted to, finally grow two inches taller. He could even turn into an eagle and fly alongside Artan – then he remembered the grotesque appearance of Murkle and Snitch after he sprayed them with a revelation potion. They had morphed into twisted versions of all of their previous forms before revealing themselves as a vicious two-headed dragon. The temptation passed. "Is there a way get rid of it?"

"Only one that I know of. The magic Orin gave you feeds on energy and uses it to create things. Now that it has taken the dragon's change magic, the only way to get rid of it is to allow your own magic to feed on it and create something from it. But you are far from ready to do that. You mustn't even consider it until you begin your training with Orin."

"So I've got to put up with it until I'm thirteen?" said Alfie.

"Perhaps longer," said Emily. "It will take time for Orin to teach you."

"How is this training even supposed to work? Orin lives six hundred years in the past!" Alfie had tried many times to will himself back into Orin's time. His birth during a magical timeslip had given him the ability to slip between present day and the year he was born, over six hundred years ago, but it was uncontrolled. He hadn't even come close to travelling back intentionally.

Emily leant forwards and said quietly, "Ashford may be able help you."

"What do you mean?" asked Alfie.

"He could teach you how to go back in time. You both share that unusual skill."

Alfie's eyes widened. "You're telling me Ashford can timeslip too? There are others, like me?"

"Very few. Ashford was born with the ability. Like you, he can travel between two time periods, hundreds of years apart."

Alfie couldn't believe that Ashford had been living with them for nearly a year and hadn't thought to share this with him.

"How—"

"I can't say any more," said Emily. "Caspian would be furious if he knew I had told you about Ashford's ability."

She glanced at her watch as she mentioned his name.

"I'm sure he'll be back soon," said Alfie.

"Of course he will," said Emily, smiling quickly. "Meanwhile, I have some experience with change magics. Maybe if I teach you to use it, you will be able to stop it manifesting itself." She took Alfie's cup and put it aside. "Show me."

Alfie stared at her. "But I didn't use it on purpose. It just happened. I don't know how to use it."

"Have you tried?"

Alfie shook his head.

"Well then, try."

Alfie couldn't believe that Emily expected him to be able to use Murkle and Snitch's magic at will, but it didn't sound as though she was going to take no for an answer.

"What do I do?" he asked.

"Find where it lies inside you and wake it."

Archie tried to relax and follow Emily's instructions. He closed his eyes and remembered the sensation of power that had built up inside him before he used the ancient magic against Murkle

61

and Snitch. He turned his mind inwards and searched for that feeling. Just as he was starting to feel irritated, he felt it – the ancient magic coiled like a snake inside his chest. He could sense something smaller there with it, the change magic caught in its coils. Alfie focused on it and felt it slowly come awake, sending a slight tingle through every nerve in his body.

"Good. Now, let it flow through you." Emily's words floated on the edge of Archie's hearing. "Let's try something simple. Your skin. Let's see if you can turn it blue."

"I don't know how."

"Focus. Find a way."

"But, I—"

"Do it. Become blue."

Alfie sighed irritably and focused hard on the colour blue.

"You're trying too hard," said Emily. "Imagine it just happening, rather than trying to make it happen."

Alfie relaxed a little and imagined the colour washing over him, painting his entire body, his eyelids, his fingernails, in-between his toes. He imagined it was a truth. Just as the grass was green, Alfie Bloom was blue.

"Open your eyes," said Emily softly.

Alfie blinked and looked down at his hands. "I did it," he whispered, flexing his blue fingers and pulling up the leg of his jeans to reveal a blue leg.

"You did brilliantly," smiled Emily. "That was remarkable for someone untrained. If you knew how difficult that was, you might never have managed it."

"How do I turn back?" asked Alfie, a tight feeling gripping his stomach as he imagined going back to school looking like an alien.

"I'm sure you can figure that out too."

Alfie looked down at his hands, imagining the blue washing away and the familiar flesh tones returning to his skin. He had barely begun to think it when the blue seemed to fade away, like ink soaking into his skin as his colour returned to normal.

Emily laughed. "That was amazing! You commanded it with incredible ease. Let's try something bigger. If I asked you to draw someone from memory, who would you be most confident choosing?"

Alfie didn't even have to think. "My dad."

"Excellent. Become your dad."

Turning his skin blue was one thing, but Alfie

couldn't believe what Emily was asking "But how? Where do I even start?"

"Let's just try getting his head right," said Emily. "A full body transformation is a bit much for a first try. This sort of magic should allow you to change your clothes too, but that's far too advanced. Now, imagine your face changing to become your father's."

Alfie stayed silent. What Emily was asking seemed impossible, but he didn't want to let her down by not even trying. He took a deep breath and let it out slowly as he closed his eyes and imagined his dad's face. He already shared some of his dad's features, so first he imagined becoming an older version of himself with a longer face, broader chin, and a more defined jaw. It was much more difficult that turning his skin blue; there were so many little details to remember.

"Great work," said Emily. "Keep going."

Alfie imagined his nose growing a little larger, his eyes turning brown and little laughter lines appearing at their edges. It felt as though his skin was being gently pulled and stretched. His chin itched slightly. He touched it and jumped when it felt bristly, as though he needed to start shaving. Maybe he could do this after all! He opened his eyes.

"A brilliant start," said Emily, "You even managed the eye colour. But I can see you're getting tired. Let's leave it there."

Alfie shook his head. He didn't mean to ignore Emily, but he knew he was getting close; he just wasn't trying hard enough. His scalp tingled as he imagined his hair turning from red-brown to black with little grey flecks around his temples.

"Excellent, Alfie, but stop now. This is far more than I expected already."

Her words floated just on the edge of Alfie's hearing as he focused on the transformation. Maybe he could grow a little too. His clothes began to feel tighter. He looked down at his feet. They definitely seemed further away. Excited by this, he imagined sending out a message to every particle in his body, demanding that it camouflage itself. It was starting to happen, he was sure of it.

"Stop! Stop NOW!"

The sharp tone in Emily's voice shattered Archie's concentration. He blinked up at her in surprise. Emily was staring at him, her face a picture of shock and concern.

"Sorry. I thought I nearly had it." Emily was still staring at him, so he added, "I just wanted to keep trying. I didn't mean to make you mad."

Emily handed him her powder compact.

Alfie stared into the mirror in horror. He had changed all right. He had his dad's hair, stubble, and most of his features, but they were hideously distorted – green and scaly. He raised his hand to his face and let out a scream as he saw long black claws instead of fingers. Emily caught him as his legs gave way. She guided him to a chair.

"What's happening to me?" He was shaking with shock at the sight of his own monstrous face.

"Breathe," said Emily, gently patting his hand. "It's diminishing."

Archie looked back at the mirror and let out a shuddery gasp of relief to see his skin losing the hideous green scales and fading back into flesh.

"I'm sorry, Alfie. The change magic resided in a dragon for hundreds of years," said Emily. "When you tried to force it to work, it started to take the shape it knows the best. It will take patience and great strength of will to teach it new forms."

"I don't want to," said Alfie, still shaken from his transformation into a mutant dragon.

"You don't have to," said Emily. "But if you want to keep it under control, you should practise with it. It could be a long time until you get rid of it, and if it manifests itself in the meantime, you can at least control it."

Alfie continued to breathe calmly and shuddered with relief as he risked another look in the mirror and saw his own face looking back at him.

"Hey, Al," said Amy, sticking her head around the door of the library. "Your granny brought food up from the farm and was wondering if Emily is staying for dinner? Whoa, you look a bit green around the gills, are you OK?"

"Is that the time?" said Emily, checking her watch and leaping to her feet to divert attention from Alfie as his skin finished returning to its natural colour. "I'm afraid I have to leave. Ashford, he still isn't back?"

"No sign yet," said Amy as they headed out of the library.

"Promise me you'll make sure he calls me as soon as he returns?" said Emily as they said goodbye in the courtyard.

"Promise," said Alfie. He waved as Emily turned her car around, and she beeped as she drove away over the drawbridge.

"Robin's gone and your dad's getting cleaned up," said Amy. "I don't know what they were making in the workshop, but they were covered in soot."

"Just in time to set the table," said Granny as they went back inside. "Gracie sent the tastiest roast chicken I've ever smelt!"

"With home-made gravy? And roasties?" asked Alfie, his mouth watering as he hurried into the Great Hall after her with plates and cutlery.

Alfie's dad had told Granny and the twins' parents about the kidnapping and release of Ashford, but he had left out a few important details such as the elves, the arrow, the fact it happened in the castle, and that the police hadn't been called. They had jumped to their own conclusion that it had been a case of mistaken identity and everyone was happy to leave it that way.

Alfie's dad joined them as they sat down to the feast the twins' mum had sent up with Granny. Alfie barely had time to swallow his first bite when the *boom-boom-boom* of the castle's door knocker echoed from the entrance hall.

Alfie raced Amy to the door.

"Ashford!" Alfie cried, flinging his arms around the butler's waist, hardly pausing to wonder at the loose pinstriped trousers, wellies and ugly Hawaiian shirt he was wearing.

6

The Fair Folk

Ashford was hustled into the Great Hall and pushed into a seat at the table as Granny piled his plate high with food.

"After this we should take you to hospital to get your shoulder looked at," said Alfie's dad, as the butler tore a leg from the roast chicken.

"Aches a little, but they did a great job patching me up," said Ashford as he picked the chicken leg clean.

"You hurt your shoulder?" said Granny, looking around the table. "And no one thought to mention it? Maybe I should take a look. . ."

"No need," said Ashford quickly. "It's almost completely healed."

Alfie wondered if Ashford was lying so that Granny wouldn't be shocked at the wound, but then he remembered the salve the healers had used at Muninn and Bone's offices. It had cleared up his bruises in no time. Perhaps the elves had something even better. He hoped so; that would mean that Ashford hadn't spent the last couple of days in agony, as he had been imagining.

"So, you're OK?" said Alfie, not wanting to ask too much in front of Granny.

"They looked after me well," said Ashford as he reached out to tear more meat from the chicken. "Better than I deserved."

"You can't mean that." Alfie wondered if Ashford felt guilty over his career as a thief "You didn't deserve that. Not at all!"

"How did you get back here?" asked Amy.

"Let's leave the questions for now," said Granny as the butler shovelled more food into his mouth. "Can't you see he's ravenous? We're very happy you're home, Ashford."

Robin was back at the castle the next morning to work on his mysterious project with Alfie's dad. He was disappointed not to see Ashford, but the butler was spending the day in bed to recover from his ordeal. Alfie had tried to get him to call Emily, but Ashford had said that he was too tired and would ring her later. Alfie could understand that, but hoped he would call her soon. She had been so worried about him.

"Do you think he's avoiding talking to her?" he asked Amy.

"Didn't you say they might be going out with each other?" she replied. "Maybe he's embarrassed over getting kidnapped, or worried she'll be angry at him for nearly leading the elves straight to your talisman?"

In the end, Alfie phoned Emily himself to let her know that Ashford was safely home.

"He doesn't want to talk to me?" said Emily, unable to hide the hurt in her voice.

"He's been through a lot," said Alfie, guilt writhing in his stomach. "He said he'll speak to you when he's feeling better."

"OK," said Emily. "But Caspian returns from a client meeting in feudal Japan the day after tomorrow and he will want to see Ashford as soon as he returns. Could you let him know?"

"I will."

Alfie rubbed his neck uneasily as he put down the phone. He hoped Ashford would want to speak to her soon. He was obviously more affected by his ordeal than he was letting on and could probably use someone to talk to.

Robin went out with Alfie's dad to buy more materials for whatever they were making in the workshop. Alfie guessed that it involved melting down metal. Heat was pouring out of the room where the forge had been set up and his dad and cousin were wearing thick leather aprons and gloves.

Granny had insisted that Alfie and Amy head down to the farm that morning to help with the shearing. Alfie guessed it was so that they wouldn't bother Ashford with questions. As they walked down to the farm he noticed stalls going up in the marketplace.

"Of course! It's the Beltane festival tomorrow," he told Amy.

"The what?"

"It's a fire festival the village holds every year to mark the beginning of summer." Alfie had hardly given it a thought, but now that Ashford was home he couldn't wait to join in the fun. "You're going to love it. It doesn't usually fall in the school holidays, but it's really late this year."

Down on the farm, Granny was already in her

overalls shearing sheep with Uncle Herb. Alfie and Amy were immediately put to work. As an experienced farmhand, Madeleine was daubing insect repellent on to the sheeps' backs after they had been shorn. Alfie and Amy ended up with the slightly easier task of binding and bagging fleeces as Granny and Uncle Herb sheared them from the sheep, which were strangely placid under their skilful hands.

"Granny," said Alfie as the last of the fleece she was shearing fell to the ground. "What do you know about elves?"

Granny's right eyebrow rose as she looked shrewdly at the trio. The sheep in front of her came out of its trance and bounded happily across the barn to be chased down by Madeleine.

"You wouldn't be poking fun at your old granny now, would you?"

"No, Mrs Merryweather," said Amy earnestly. "Alfie says your stories are great. We thought you might know one about elves."

Granny nodded approvingly at Alfie. "Well, he wouldn't be wrong," she smiled. "And call me Granny, dear. Only doctors and dentists call me Mrs Merryweather and I don't need reminding of either of those any time soon." She took hold of the bucking sheep Madeleine had led over to her and whispered a few words in its ear. It calmed down immediately and she flipped it on to its back and began shearing its stomach.

"So, you want to know about the Fair Folk, as my grandpa used to call them. Well I never saw an elf, but I've seen the havoc their sprites can wreak with my own two eyes."

"What are sprites?" asked Alfie as Amy bound the rolled fleece he was holding tightly.

"Nasty little things. Elves, pixies, sprites – they all live in the same realm. But elves have no time for mischief; they're more likely to steal people away into their realm. Sprites are a different story. Whenever anything went wrong on my grandpa's farm he said that the sprites had a hand in it. One year his neighbour built a road through a lis on the next farm over—"

"A what?" asked Alfie.

"A lis, as I was about to tell you, is a mound with a raised earth bank around it. Grandma said they were the remains of ancient dwellings, but Grandpa told me they were fairy mounds: entrances to the land of the Fair Folk."

Alfie and Amy had stopped rolling fleeces as they drank in Granny's words.

"Keep working," said Uncle Herb. "Stories don't come free."

"There was something unnatural about that lis," continued Granny. "The air around it always felt charged, as though the whole place was awake and watching. Well, after Bill Duffy bulldozed it there was no good news on any farm around it. Potatoes got blight, milk curdled in the pails, chickens stopped laying and the vet was always treating one sick animal or another. My grandparents sold the farm in the end. Mum said they were getting a bit too old to manage it, but I know that wasn't the reason." She leant towards Alfie and Amy, eyes wide as she whispered, "It was because old Bill angered the Fair Folk."

Even the sheep were silent as Granny finished her story. The barn was so quiet that Alfie almost leapt out of his skin when the ewe Madeleine was holding let out a loud *BAAAA*.

"Are you going to tell them you made that up, or are you going to let them have nightmares for weeks?" laughed Uncle Herb.

"Don't give me that cheek, my boy!" said Granny, giving him a smart rap across the knuckles. "It's as true as any tale I've ever told. Everyone my age knows the story of Thomas

Skelderskew who went nine times widdershins around a ring of toadstools down on Fairy Cross Plain. He hasn't been seen in over a hundred years. And don't let that give you any ideas, Madeleine Merryweather. Stories or not, there are some things you don't mess with."

Alfie had been thinking about Ashford. "If someone was taken by the elves and then came back, would they be OK? I mean, would they be the same as before they were taken?"

"Only a few have ever returned in all the tales I've heard," said Granny. "And they were changed. Most of them spent their whole lives trying to return to the land of the Fair Folk. Now, less talking, more tidying." She grinned as she stood up, collected her shearing tools and headed for the storage cupboard.

"Do you think that was all true?" Alfie asked Madeleine as they stacked the fleeces.

"Maybe a bit of it. That's the thing with Granny's stories – you're never sure where to look for the truth."

Alfie hoped that Granny was wrong, but Ashford did seem different. What if he tried to find a way back to his kidnappers?

*

Robin had already left when Alfie and Amy got back to the castle. Alfie's dad was heading down to the library to find more books on ironworking. As Amy went off to wash the wool fluff from her hair, Alfie descended the little staircase behind a panel in the entrance hall to visit Ashford. He had only seen the butler's room once before when he was borrowing some watercolour paints. It had been very neat and orderly, the walls covered in colourful landscapes Ashford had made of the castle and the surrounding countryside. There was even a small, beautifully painted picture of Emily Fortune. However, today all of the furniture seemed to have been emptied out into the corridor outside his room.

Alfie caught his breath as he tiptoed around furniture and bedding. Had someone broken into the castle again? He peered around the door and saw the butler striding about the room stripping paintings from the wall. He was wearing trousers and a white vest. The only other time Alfie had seen him out of uniform was the night before, when he was dressed as though he'd raided someone's washing line.

"Did you want something?" asked Ashford, stopping work as he spotted Alfie standing in the doorway.

"I just wanted to make sure you're OK," said Alfie, feeling slightly awkward. "Emily said Caspian wants to see you when he gets back the day after tomorrow."

"Ha! I bet he does," laughed Ashford. "Can't keep his beak out of other folk's business."

Alfie knew Ashford and Caspian weren't best friends, but had always sensed there was a mutual respect between the two. He was very surprised to hear Ashford talking like this. Did he blame Caspian for not rescuing him?

"I'm sure it can wait, if you're not ready?" he added.

The butler seemed to sense Alfie's surprise and changed his attitude. "In two days, you say? Two days will be fine. I'll be ready by then." He took down the portrait of Emily. "Just having a spring clean," he smiled. "I thought it might help clear my mind."

Alfie took the portrait from Ashford and laid it carefully on the desk in the hall as the butler continued turning his room upside down.

"Do you need any help with..." Alfie waved his hands around at the disorder, "... all this?"

"No need," said Ashford, opening a chest and throwing his clothes out on to the floor. "You can run along now."

Alfie trudged back up the stairs, biting his lip as he remembered what Granny had said about strange things happening to the minds of those who returned from the realm of the elves.

That evening Ashford announced that he was too tired to eat dinner with everyone after his spring cleaning.

"Is he OK?" asked Amy after they'd watched the butler help himself to the rest of the chicken from the night before and take it down to eat alone in his room. "Gran went a bit weird for a couple of weeks after someone stole her purse in the street last year. The doctor said it was post-traumatic stress. I bet that's what Ash has. Maybe he should see a doctor?"

"I don't think he'll agree to that," said Alfie. "Hopefully Caspian can get help for him."

Although Ashford wasn't joining them for dinner, there was an extra person at the table. Alfie's dad had bumped into Alfie's head teacher, Miss Reynard, in the village and invited her to the castle for dinner. Alfie was surprised. His dad was usually awkward around new people, but he seemed to be talking and laughing with Miss Reynard quite easily. He was pleased his dad was making friends, especially with his favourite teacher. He was even more pleased that his dad had ordered Indian food rather than cooking, which meant that she wouldn't be put off coming for dinner again.

"Is she your dad's girlfriend?" whispered Amy, pinching the rest of Alfie's roti and using it to mop up her curry.

"Don't be daft," said Alfie, almost dropping his spoon. "They're just friends."

"Oh, OK." She grinned and made little quotation marks in the air with her fingers. "Just friends."

"Grow up," said Alfie, slapping her hand away as she reached for his last onion bhaji. It had been several years since his mum had died and he had never imagined his dad with anyone else. He squirrelled the idea away to explore later when he had time to think about how it made him feel. Nevertheless, he found himself watching his dad and teacher a little more carefully as they chattered away on the other side of the table.

"So, Alfie," said Miss Reynard, suddenly meeting his eyes. "How is the exploring going? Don't tell me you've investigated every inch of this place already?"

"We've found quite a bit," said Alfie. "Most of

the rooms on the official plans anyway. Apparently there's loads of stuff that isn't marked on there."

"Like the eastern tower," interrupted Amy. "We can't find the way into it anywhere."

"That sounds like an adventure waiting to happen," said Miss Reynard. "Would you mind if I helped you look after dinner?"

"Not at all. Brilliant idea!" Alfie's dad chimed in so quickly that Alfie wondered if he had been looking for an excuse to keep her around a little longer.

Alfie and Amy cleared the table and washed the dishes. When they returned to the Great Hall, his dad and Miss Reynard were laying kindling in the huge fireplace.

"Hazel tells me it's tradition to relight the fire on Beltane with a flame taken from the bonfire down in the village," said Alfie's dad as Miss Reynard arranged wooden logs on top of the kindling.

"That's right," she added. "During Beltane, cattle would be driven between two fires in the belief that it would keep them free from disease for the next year. At the end of the festival everyone took a bit of the fire back into their own home."

"Did it work?" asked Alfie.

Miss Reynard shrugged. "It made them feel as

though they had some form of control over it, so what does it matter?" She wiped her hands on her dress as she finished laying the fire. "There we go – all ready for tomorrow. Now, let's find that door!"

The tower started from the third floor rather than the ground, so Alfie had figured out the most likely place for an entrance would be on that floor. He led the way to where a stone carving of two knights marked the end of the third-floor corridor. A metal bracket holding a torch was fitted to each of the carvings. Alfie realized that he had never seen them lit before. He stood a short way down the corridor and watched as his dad and teacher began to examine the carving to see if there was a way it could be made to open like a door.

"They won't find anything," he said quietly to Amy. "I've been over it dozens of times. If it is a door, there's no way to open it."

"What about your talisman?" asked Amy. "You used that to open the entrance to Orin's study, and it opens the big seal thing in the cellars. Surely it must open this door too?"

"Nope. I've been over every inch of the carving. There's nowhere for it to slot into."

"Did you try looking through the lens?"

Alfie felt his cheeks go red.

"You didn't, did you?" she laughed.

Making sure Miss Reynard was occupied with the carving, Alfie held the talisman to his eye like a monocle. He trusted his teacher, but was very careful about keeping the talisman hidden now that so many people seemed to be after it. He couldn't see anything unusual as he scrutinized the carving from a distance through the purple lens. Turning to Amy, something on the wall to his left caught his eye. In glowing ink on two bricks were written the numbers one and three. On the wall to the right were bricks bearing the numbers two and four. Now that he had seen them through the lens he noticed that their surface was a little smoother than the other bricks. He tucked the talisman back into his T-shirt.

"What did you see, Al?" asked Amy.

"Step back, Dad," Alfie called. "I think I can open it." His dad and teacher moved away from the carving as Alfie pressed each of the bricks in the order they were labelled. They moved very slightly into the wall as he pushed on them. The instant he hit the fourth the two torches held by the carved knights burst into flame. There was a faint clanking from deep within the walls. A hairline gap appeared between the two knights and they began to slide apart with a soft grating noise, coming to rest on either side of a dark entrance.

"Amazing!" said Miss Reynard. "However did you figure that out?"

"The bricks were a bit smoother than the others," said Alfie, thinking quickly. "I wondered what would happen if I pressed them."

"Very clever!" said Alfie's dad, taking one of the flaming torches from the wall and passing another to Miss Reynard. "Shall we?"

Alfie and Amy rushed through first. The flickering torches revealed a door ahead of them and the start of a spiral staircase to their left. The door led into a large round room.

"It's an armoury!" gasped Miss Reynard as their torches revealed walls lined with swords and spears. Hanging on crude wooden mannequins in the centre of the room were chain-mail shirts, each with a pair of iron gloves. Alfie knew that if Robin was there he would be telling everyone that they were called gauntlets. He pulled a pair on. They were lighter and more flexible than he expected, and the chain mail looked much easier to wear than the suits of armour in the rest of the castle. He had given up trying those on until he was at least a foot taller and a lot stronger.

"How do I look?" asked Amy, giving a twirl. She was wearing one of the mail shirts with the hood up.

"Like a weird robot," laughed Alfie.

Amy made a noise like an engine whirring and marched stiffly around the room. Alfie laughed, but secretly wondered why Orin would have so much weaponry and armour in the castle. Did the druid think that Alfie would have use of it all? The castle wasn't exactly turning out to be as safe as he had first imagined it to be.

Alfie's dad was unlocking another door. "If I'm right," he said as he turned the handle, "This should lead out on to..." he swung the door open, "Yes! The higher battlements."

Alfie rushed outside and leant over the stone wall to look down on to the lower battlements where he had hidden from Ashford the night the butler was kidnapped. "I've flown up here on Artan but have been looking for the key to that door for ages!" he whispered to Amy. "Now we know where it leads. I can't wait to show Madeleine and Robin."

The room on the next floor was filled with many different types of clothing from several continents. Miss Reynard informed them that they dated from the mid-1400s to the late 1600s.

"How wonderful!" she exclaimed as she examined embroidered Persian tunics and elaborate Italian robes from the Renaissance period. "If these belonged to Orin Hopcraft I have no idea how he got them. Hardly anyone left their region, let alone the country, in those days."

"Disguises?" whispered Amy in Alfie's ear.

"To fit in with the locals on his excursions with Artan," Alfie grinned. With a flying bearskin rug, Orin was bound to be the most widely travelled person in the Middle Ages, but he couldn't exactly tell Miss Reynard that. He promised to let Miss Reynard borrow some of the clothing for her history lessons and they continued up the stairs.

The next room was so full that they had to squeeze themselves among tables and stone pedestals holding all manner of fantastic objects from around the world. Miss Reynard rushed from item to item with such excitement that she reminded Alfie of Madeleine. There was an ornate turban, a highly detailed coloured glass goblet, pearl and jewelled necklaces and rings, and a very long silk scarf embroidered with every animal Alfie could name – and lots he couldn't.

Under many of the objects were notes written

in different languages. Miss Reynard was able to translate the ones in more recognizable languages such as French and German. "They're thank-you notes," she told Alfie. "This one, with the ruby ring, is from Charles VIII of France for healing sores on his legs. This one, with the painting of the hare, is from a German artist, thanking Orin for procuring rare coloured pigments for him."

"Look at this!" Alfie's dad called out. They joined him as he stood gazing transfixed at a small silver sparrow on a marble plinth. Each of its feathers was finely engraved with tiny details that made it look extremely true to life.

"There's a key," said Amy, picking up a small metal object from beneath it. "Do you think it can be wound up?"

Alfie found a tiny hole under one of the wings. He clicked the key into place and turned it, removing it when it could turn no more. They all watched the bird with baited breath.

"It blinked!" cried Alfie. The little bird's head suddenly twitched from side to side and then it lifted its wing and groomed the feathers beneath. When it was satisfied, it straightened up, gave its tail feathers a little shake, and then opened its tiny beak to chirrup a beautiful melody.

"Amazing," said Alfie's dad as the bird hopped from foot to foot in time with its own tune. "How does it work?"

Amy let out a little yelp as, without warning, the bird launched itself into the air, brushing her cheek with its wing tip as it whizzed past her and circled the room twice before coming back to rest on the plinth. There was a soft whirring noise as it clicked back into its original position and wound down. Alfie smiled to see the childlike wonder on his dad's face.

"Only a true genius would be able to make something like this, Alfie. He or she is a better inventor than I could ever hope to be. There's no note. I wonder if Orin built it?"

"There's something engraved here," said Alfie, squinting to make out two letters on one of the tail feathers. One was engraved over the other. "There's a D . . . and the other is . . . yes, it's an L."

"DL . . . DL. . ." his dad repeated. "Wait! Let me see that!" he almost knocked Alfie over in his haste to see the initials. His face went white and he staggered backwards. Alfie grabbed his dad's arm as his legs appeared to give out.

"I don't believe it . . . I don't believe it," he muttered between deep breaths. "It can't be."

"Will, are you OK?" asked Miss Reynard, reaching out to touch his shoulder. "What is it?"

"I have to check something." He dashed to the spiral staircase. "Wait there! I'll be back!" he called as he disappeared.

"What's got into Mr B?" asked Amy as his footsteps faded away below them.

"He usually gets like that when he suddenly thinks of a solution to something he's been working on," said Alfie, puzzled. "I've never seen him *quite* that excited before though."

They marvelled at the rest of the room's contents as they waited. Inside a long, soft roll of leather, Alfie found more weapons: two beautifully made wooden bows inlaid with a delicate silver pattern.

"They're beautiful," said Amy, lifting one of them and pulling back the string with difficulty. "Do you know how to shoot?"

Alfie shook his head. "Granny tried to teach me but I'm always twanging the inside of my elbow. These are going straight to Madeleine and Robin."

"How very kind of you," said Miss Reynard. "Just make sure they never bring them to school – even without arrows!" There was a scrambling noise on the stairs and Alfie's dad burst into the room, panting. He was holding a heavy book.

"I was right!" he laughed. "It wasn't DL, it was LD. Look!" He flipped rapidly through the pages of the book and, below a sketch, he pointed to the two letters entwined in the same way. Alfie suddenly understood. It was his dad's favourite book. They had pored over its pictures together many times. They were by his dad's favourite artist and inventor. He stared wide-eyed at his dad as they both started to laugh in amazement.

"What?" said Amy. "Who's LD?"

Miss Reynard was a bit quicker on the uptake as she showed Amy the book cover.

"No. *Way!*" said Amy. "*Leonardo da Vinci?*"

"It has to be," Alfie's dad flipped to a page featuring diagrams of a mechanical lion. "He presented this to the king of France in 1515. It walked on its own and its chest opened to reveal a bunch of lilies."

"He built several clockwork devices before this," said Miss Reynard, sounding just as excited herself. "One was a robotic knight in armour that could move its arms and sit down." Alfie noticed his dad gaze at Miss Reynard as though this was the most wonderful thing she could have said. Alfie felt a little spark of jealousy, but it vanished under the waves of his dad's almost delirious happiness at the little bird created by da Vinci himself.

"How Orin ended up with a castle of such wonders is completely beyond me," said Miss Reynard. "If only we could speak to him. What adventures he must have had!"

"If only there was a way," smiled Alfie.

7

Beltane

The twins came up to the castle early the following day. Madeleine cried out with delight as Alfie presented her with one of the bows he had found in the eastern tower. She nocked an arrow and drew back the string in one fluid movement.

"Our bows are competition quality, but *these*! These are amazing!"

"Thank you *so* much, Alfie," said Robin, examining his gift. "Are you *sure* you want to give these to us?"

"Shhh!" Madeleine clutched her bow close to her chest. "If he wants it back, he'll have to fight me for it."

"No need for that," said Alfie quickly. "I'm no good with those things anyway." Granny had been training the twins in archery since they were very young, but even so, they had an almost unnatural talent for it.

Everyone was very excited about the Beltane celebration that was taking place that evening. Alfie's dad had gone down to the village to help Granny set up stands. He hadn't seemed to want to leave the little bird that had been constructed by his hero. Alfie had moved it down to the Great Hall so that every visitor to the castle could see it, which resulted in his dad's cornflakes turning to mush in his bowl as he admired it over breakfast.

There was plenty of time before they had to get ready for the festival, so Alfie decided to show the twins the discoveries of the night before.

"Hey, Ash," said Amy as they passed the butler emerging from his room. "We're going up the eastern tower. Alfie found the way in. Fancy joining us?"

"I'll give it a miss," said Ashford, heading for the kitchen. He was wearing stripy pyjamas with dress shoes and had a cravat tied in a bow around his neck.

Alfie felt the others giving him a sideways look. Amy nudged him to say something.

"Ashford, are you OK?"

The butler stopped and looked at Alfie, his head tilted quizzically.

"It's just that you're dressed..." he tailed off, unsure of how to say it.

"Like a total weirdo!" finished Madeleine, earning herself a sharp glance from Robin.

Ashford looked down as though seeing his clothes for the first time.

"Ahh, I see what you mean," he laughed.

"Do you need any, you know ... help?" asked Alfie.

"Help?" repeated Ashford, eyebrows knitted together. "Ohhh, *that* kind of help." He tapped his finger on the side of his head. "No, I'm as sane as I've ever been, thanks." He grinned and turned to leave, then paused.

"Actually, there is something you might be able to help with. You've probably noticed that my memory hasn't been the same since I got back. I've lost something quite valuable. For the life of me, I can't figure out where it is."

"We'll help you look!" said Madeleine immediately. "What is it? Is it metal? I've got a metal detector; I'll go get it!"

"No, no!" said Ashford quickly as Madeleine rushed for the door. "It's private. A gift ... for Emily. I was only wondering if you have any ideas about where I might have stored it?"

Alfie was glad that Ashford was going to make things up with Emily. He thought hard. "Maybe you left it in one of the drawers in the kitchens. Or have you tried the undercroft? You store lots of things down there."

"Yes. The undercroft," said Ashford, beaming. "I'll start there." He bounded away into the kitchens.

"He's really not quite right, is he?" asked Amy worriedly.

"Maybe he hit his head or something when they shot him," said Robin. "Or the elves might have drugged him, or brainwashed him; that's why he's not even angry at them."

"He needs a doctor," said Alfie, biting his lip at the thought of Ashford being brainwashed. "But I don't think the one in the village would know what to do. Hopefully Caspian will take him to one of their healers when he comes tomorrow."

Alfie led the way up to the tower. The twins spent hours looking through the treasures and trying on costumes and armour.

The upper floors had gone unexplored after the excitement of the silver sparrow. As they made their way up through the tower, Alfie was disappointed to find out that the rest of the rooms were empty. Chalked on the wooden floorboards of the room above Orin's treasures was a message.

"*Do not store anything above this room*," read Alfie. "That's weird, I wonder why?"

Every room above that one was completely empty, even though the rooms below were so full it would have made sense to distribute the contents throughout the tower.

From the very top they could look down over Hexbridge.

"What's that they're setting up in the village hall car park?" Alfie asked, squinting down at the unmistakably human shape that was being constructed from long thin strips of wood. A little figure that he assumed was Granny directed from a distance.

"That's the wicker man," said Robin.

"What's it for?"

"We burn it at sunset. It's an old tradition, to ensure a good harvest, or something like that. Every year Jimmy Feeney tells everyone that they burned people inside them hundreds of years ago, but I asked Miss Reynard and she said that's just a load of old rubbish the Romans made up. Me and Madeleine are part of the ceremony this year."

"What are you doing?" asked Alfie.

"You'll see," said Robin. "These bows you gave us should come in handy for it." Alfie was intrigued.

"Speaking of the festival," said Madeleine. "We'd better get ready!"

It didn't take long to get changed. Aunt Grace loved making costumes and had put together four simple green-and-yellow tunics for them to wear. They pulled these on over their jeans and T-shirts and began face-painting. Aunt Grace had only supplied one colour for them to paint with. Blue.

"What is this stuff?" asked Amy as she dipped a brush into the paint and trailed spirals on to the side of Madeleine's face.

"Woad," replied Robin, painting a blue mask across his face and eyelids. "It was used as a dye in medieval times. The Picts painted their faces and bodies with it. I hope Mum didn't use as much raw dye this time. Last year it took days to come off."

"OK, I'll do yours now," said Madeleine, admiring the pattern Amy had painted.

"No need." Amy dipped three fingers into the pot of paint and pulled them down her cheeks and chin in three blue lines. Alfie thought Madeleine looked a little disappointed, but as usual, even in a tunic and face paint, Amy managed to look effortlessly cool.

"How about you, Al?" she asked, waggling her blue fingers in front of his face.

"I'm good," said Alfie, a mischievous idea creeping into his head. "Want to see something really cool?" He had been thinking about Emily's words more and more. He hadn't had the nightmares since practising with the change magic. Perhaps it did make sense to take control of it before it took control of him. He concentrated, recreating the blue skin experiment he had done with Emily. He knew it was working when the others all leapt away from him.

"Whoa! What are you doing?" cried Amy.

"*How* are you doing it?" gasped Robin, cautiously approaching Alfie to stare at his pores.

Madeleine maintained her distance, her hand on a candlestick ready to throw it at Alfie if necessary.

"When I fought Murkle and Snitch in their dragon form, the magic Orin hid inside me stole their power to change shape."

"So it's in you now?" said Robin. "You can

change form like they could? Alfie, this is unbelievable."

"So you could become a dragon too?" said Madeleine. "Do it, Alfie. Do it!"

"That's one form I'm *definitely* not going to try," said Alfie quickly. He told them about the dreams and occasions the dragon scales had manifested.

"Urgh. Well, at least it isn't turning you into Murkle or Snitch," said Madeleine.

"So, what else can you do, Al?" asked Amy.

Alfie was made to turn every single colour the others could think of. He went on to amaze them by mimicking each of their faces, but was careful not to push himself too hard after the incident with the scales. It was weird to feel the hair growing from his scalp and flowing down over his shoulders as he transformed his face into Amy's.

"So, yeah," he said, flicking back the hair as he tried to imitate Amy's voice. "It's like, sooo hard being this awesome."

"Really?" said Amy, hands on her hips. "You're *wearing my face* and that was still the worst impression ever. Seriously. The worst!"

"It was a bit weird," said Robin. "Come on, change back. We need to go down to the village."

Alfie saw Ashford in the kitchens as they

passed through the entrance hall. He had pulled everything out of all the drawers and moved on to the kitchen cabinets.

"Are you still looking for Emily's present, Ashford?" asked Alfie.

"Looking for what?" Ashford quickly pulled his head out of a cupboard. "Oh, no-no. Still spring-cleaning, clearing up for Beltane."

"I don't think you should be working yet. Why don't you come to the festival with us?"

"Perhaps later," said Ashford absent-mindedly as he pulled canisters of rice and flour out of the cupboards and began to sift through them. "Lots to do here."

"O-kaaaay, well … we might see you there then?" said Alfie, exchanging a concerned look with the others as they left the castle.

"That's it," he whispered. "I'm calling Emily and Caspian as soon as we get back. This is getting too weird."

They could hear music and the jingling bells of morris dancers as they headed down the hill. Alfie was proud of the spiral designs he had imagined on to his face. He had felt a little self-conscious in his costume, but if anything their outfits looked tame compared to the fantastic costumes some of the villagers were wearing. Many faces were painted blue, but Alfie could also see lots of green, white, red and multicoloured faces too. Some people had ivy and flowers wound through their hair; others wore flowing cloaks and headdresses. Several men had stripped to the waist and painted their chests with large blue swirls.

Alfie saw lots of school friends from Wyrmwald House enjoying the festivities. Jimmy Feeney was running a hog-roast stand with his dad, and he made sure Alfie got an extra helping of crackling. Madeleine's best friend, Holly Okoye, waved to them from where she was enjoying a picnic on the green with her family. Alfie even caught sight of arrogant Edward Snoddington and Hugo Pugsley, and he carefully avoided them as he moved through the crowd.

Delicious scents wafted on the breeze. Alfie recognized cinnamon, freshly baked bread and cakes. From Gertie Entwhistle's colourful sweet stall wafted chocolate and the rose scent of Turkish delight. The many craft and food stalls that lined the square were draped in spring-coloured fabrics tied with bunches of flowers.

Alfie found his dad sitting on a hay bale tapping his feet to the music. He was watching people skipping around the maypole, expertly weaving coloured ribbons round it as they danced.

"You can have the rest of these if you don't tell your granny where I am," he said, offering Alfie a bag of what looked like flat buttery scones. "Bannock cakes. Freshly baked," he said, wiping crumbs from his tunic. "Ooh look, they're lighting the fires."

It was starting to get darker now and everyone cheered as two bonfires flared up to light the square. A group of drummers began to pound out a beat that had everyone clapping along as a troupe of dancers performed acrobatics.

Alfie thought the dances and performances were starting to get much more interesting now that it was getting dark. Everything seemed to involve fire. Jugglers sent flaming torches spinning across the square to each other, always catching them at the right end. Fire-eaters appeared to swallow flames and then spat jets of fire from their mouths like dragons.

Amy let out an appreciative whistle as a woman threw back her head and blew a cloud of flames high into the air.

"Don't get any ideas," said Alfie's dad quickly. "Those people know exactly what they are doing. Although *why* they're doing it is a mystery to me!"

After the fire-eating there was a long drum roll as a woman dressed in red and orange took up position in front of a path of burning coals. Another performer poured a glass of water on to the coal and there was a loud hiss and a cloud of steam.

"She's not going to walk on them, is she?" said Alfie as the woman took off her sandals. Before his dad could answer she had walked straight across the glowing coals. The crowd burst into applause as she displayed the unmarked soles of her feet before flipping forwards and crossing back to the other side on her hands.

"It's not as impressive as you think," Alfie's dad told him over the applause. "Coal is a very poor conductor of heat and the layer of ash on top is a good insulator. Notice she doesn't put her feet or hands down for longer than a second? There isn't time for the heat to pass into her skin and burn it. Watch."

The woman had just called out for a volunteer. Before Alfie knew what was happening, his dad was over there untying his shoes and turning up his jeans.

"I don't believe it!" said Madeleine. "Uncle Will is going to fire-walk?" Alfie hoped his dad knew what he was doing.

The drum roll started again. The fire-walker took Alfie's dad's hand and walked alongside him as he strode briskly across the coals, smiling all the way. Everyone applauded and whistled as he reached the other side and dusted the ash from his feet.

"You were brilliant, Mr B!" said Amy as he rejoined them.

"Nothing to it," he grinned, casting an eye over Alfie's shoulder. Alfie turned to see Miss Reynard a couple of metres away, clapping louder than anyone else. Amy tapped the side of her nose and Alfie suddenly realized why his dad had volunteered for the daring challenge.

"THIS WAY, EVERYONE," Granny called through her megaphone.

"I hate it when she uses that thing!" said Robin, as Granny's helpers herded the crowd into the village hall car park. At the far end was the wicker man, standing the height of five men.

"The votes for the May Queen have been counted," called Granny's amplified voice. "But before we crown her, write down your hopes for the coming year and tuck them into the wicker man."

"Here," said Madeleine, handing Alfie some

paper. "I'm writing 'I hope we don't get Mr Smeadon for history classes in September'."

"I'm hoping Gran gets better soon, and lets me come to stay for the summer holidays," said Amy.

"I hope that we get really clear skies so that I can see the meteor showers in June," said Robin, scribbling away.

Alfie thought for a few moments, then wrote simply:

I hope Ashford is OK

"Alfie, come here a minute," called Granny as he ran over to the wicker man.

"I'll put your paper in," said Amy. Alfie handed it to her and then rushed back to see what his gran wanted. She was holding the gold-painted holly crown he had worn when he was crowned Winter King during the Samhain festival in October.

"You'll need this," she said, plonking it on his head. "And this." She handed him a circle of ivy intertwined with yellow mayflowers. "When I announce the May Queen, you crown her with this and give her a kiss."

"WHAT?" Alfie cried.

"Just on the cheek," said Granny "And don't give

me that look. The Winter King always crowns the May Queen and my grandson isn't going to break hundreds of years of tradition."

"Yes, but do I have to—" his voice was drowned out as Granny lifted her megaphone again and announced:

"Thank you all for sharing in our Beltane celebration. To mark the end of winter and the beginning of summer, our Winter King will now crown this year's May Queen, who is..." she paused dramatically. "Holly Okoye!"

Madeleine clapped and cheered the loudest as Holly climbed on to the little makeshift stage. She was wearing a bright yellow dress and had painted green ivy leaves and flowers on to the side of her face and arms. Alfie took a deep breath and planted the crown rather clumsily on her head.

"Thanks, Alfie," grinned Holly, pushing the crown up out of her eyes. He considered leaving it at that, but could feel Granny's eyes boring into him. He gave Holly's cheek the quickest peck he could then leapt back off the stage to laughter and applause from the gathered crowd. Granny gave him a look that said *I guess that will have to do*, and then lifted the megaphone.

"Now, if I can ask everyone to keep to this

side of the car park, the May Queen will start the countdown for the lighting of the wicker man."

Uncle Herb walked up to the stage carrying a flaming torch. Holly began the countdown and Madeleine and Robin stepped forwards, arrows notched to the bows Alfie had given them. There was some sort of wadding around the ends of the arrows that caught fire as soon as the twins touched it to the torch.

"Three ... two ... one," counted Holly. The twins let loose their arrows. Alfie and Amy stood together, watching the flaming arrows fly through the air to thud into the chest of the wicker figure. The crown roared as it burst into flame. The music began again in the village square and people started to pair up and dance.

"Not bad," said a voice. It took Alfie a few seconds to recognize the green painted man behind them as Ashford. He was wearing one of the green curtains from his room as a robe. He pointed at the wicker man. "But shouldn't it be filled with people?"

Alfie laughed. "Robin already told us that's a lie the Romans started. Glad you could make it."

"How did the spring cleaning go, Ash?" asked Amy.

"I'm done with that," said Ashford. "It sounded

like more fun down here." He gave an exaggerated bow. "May I have this dance?" Before Amy could answer Ashford was whirling her around the marketplace with the other dancers, swapping partners quickly from Amy to Aunt Grace to Holly's mum to Gertie Entwhistle to Miss Reynard. Alfie smiled to see the butler out of the castle and enjoying himself.

As the wicker man crumbled to ash, the food stalls finally began to pack up, and people started to drift merrily home. All of the Merryweathers were staying over at the castle that night, but the adults were taking ages clearing up and talking to the stragglers in the square. Alfie was getting very bored as they sat on the hay bales and waited.

"How about I take the kids back to the castle while you finish up here?" suggested Ashford.

"Kids!" grumbled Amy.

"That would be great. Thanks, Ashford," said Alfie's dad, looking as though he longed to escape with them. "We'll be up as soon as we're done here."

"Remember to light the fire in the castle," said Miss Reynard. She lit a torch from the dying flames of the bonfire and handed it to Alfie. They took turns to carry it as Ashford hurried them up the hill. Little sparks trailed through the night behind them. Ashford took Alfie's keys and unlocked the castle door. Once everyone was inside he clicked the tag on the key ring that drew up the drawbridge and brought the portcullis clanking down.

"Shouldn't we leave that open for Dad and the others?" asked Alfie, looking from the sealed entrance to the butler.

"After what happened to me, I'm not taking any chances," said Ashford. Alfie could understand the butler being overly security conscious, but the portal was sealed and the elves had let him go. An uneasy feeling churned in Alfie's stomach. Who was Ashford really trying to keep out – or in?

Passing the kitchen, Alfie noticed that it was still in complete disarray and covered in Ashford's floury foot and handprints. The butler had never left even a spoon out of place before. Taking the torch into the Great Hall, Alfie touched it to the kindling in the fireplace. The fire flared quickly, but its warmth didn't cheer him. Robin caught his eye; he seemed to sense something wasn't right too.

"You found this in the tower?" said Ashford, perching on the table and tapping his fingers on the little da Vinci bird.

"Yeah!" said Madeleine. "There's so much cool stuff in there. You should see it all."

"Yes, I think I'd like to," said Ashford, rubbing his hands together.

"It's getting late, Maddie," said Alfie quickly. There was something greedy about the look in Ashford's eyes. "I think tomorrow would be better."

"It's barely dusk," said Ashford. He hopped off the table. "Let's go." There was something of a command in his voice that Alfie didn't like at all. Amy and Robin had noticed it too and were making no moves to follow. Maybe the elves really *had* brainwashed him. Alfie touched his hand involuntarily to the talisman under his tunic as he always did when he felt nervous. He regretted it instantly.

"What have you got there?" asked the butler. Alfie immediately pulled his hand away and stepped back. Amy and the twins closed in protectively on either side of Alfie as the butler walked slowly towards him.

"If you were yourself, you would know," said Alfie. "So I'm thinking there's something weird going on here."

Ashford kept coming towards him. There was something wild, almost feral, about his face. Alfie

110

backed up until the heat of the fireplace kept them from going any further.

"Ashford, you're not yourself," said Alfie. "I think the elves did something to you. Let me call Emily and Caspian. They can help you." He made a step in the direction of the door.

"Stay!" commanded Ashford. "The only person that can help is standing right in front of me." The heat from the fire was making the paint on Amy and the twins' faces run as they began to sweat, but the patterns on Alfie's skin stayed fixed. His eyes flicked to Ashford's perfect green skin and his heart gave a nasty jolt as he realized what it meant.

"That's not paint. Is it?"

Ashford let out a shrill little laugh. "And I thought you were all dimwits," he laughed. Something shimmered around him and suddenly they weren't looking at Ashford any more. A thin, green-skinned man with sharp features and a crooked smile stood before them, his wide yellow eyes and sharp little teeth glinting in the firelight.

8

The Queen's Lieutenant

"Didn't expect that, did you?" The strange green man reached out, fast as lightning, and snatched the talisman from Alfie's neck. He capered round the room with it, laughing hysterically.

"The lens. You had it all along. And here I thought it would be locked away like the precious jewel it is!"

"What did you do to Ashford?" cried Alfie. "Where is he?"

"In our realm," cackled the man. "Where he's been since we took him."

Alfie's heart dropped. Ashford was still a prisoner. How could he possibly have believed otherwise?

"You're an elf?" said Robin as the man continued to dance around the hall, leaping over furniture in glee.

"Elf!" he spat. "I'm a sprite, you fool!"

"Get him!" shouted Madeleine, racing towards the sprite before anyone could stop her. He leapt to one side, caught her and flipped her over his shoulder where she kicked her legs and hammered her fists uselessly on his back.

"Nice meeting you all," he cackled. "But I must be going. The Queen has waited too long for this to be returned." He sprang away towards the courtyard, Madeleine bouncing over his shoulder like a rag doll.

The sprite moved like lightning, reaching the oak tree by the time Alfie made it to the front door, Amy hot on his heels. The sprite dropped Madeleine and snaked an arm around her neck, holding her in a grip so tight she couldn't even turn to bite him, much as she tried.

"Move and I'll snap her neck!" he shouted. With his free hand he placed the talisman into one of indentations on the metal bands around the tree and turned it with his index finger, careful to avoid touching the iron itself.

"Don't open that," shouted Alfie, as the first band fell away.

"Or what?" laughed the sprite. "I didn't think Caspian would seal off my way back, but how priceless that the lens is part of the key! When you locked me up in that cage I didn't think I'd get the portal open by Beltane," the second band fell away. "But we're just in time."

"What are you talking about?" Alfie shouted. "We didn't lock you up!"

Amy grabbed Alfie's shoulder. "The mouse!" she cried. "It was him!" The last band fell away and the sprite laughed with delight. "We should have let Galileo eat you!" she shouted.

"All coming together for you, is it?" smirked the sprite. "They left me here in mouse form in case Ashford was lying about the location of the lens. When you set me free from the cage, I sent word to the Queen of my plan to return to you as Ashford. She will be so pleased with me when I return the lens to her!"

He passed the talisman into the hand that held Madeleine, placed his fingers on the trunk of the tree, and began an incantation. Alfie recognized it as the same language spoken by the elves that had taken Ashford. A long vertical line appeared in the trunk, blue light spilling out as it opened wider. Caspian's ravens launched themselves from the castle walls, one flying away as the others began to circle the oak, cawing loudly.

"LET HER GO!" Alfie nearly leapt out of his skin as Robin's voice bellowed out from behind him. He was silhouetted against the lit doorway of the castle, bow raised and arrow notched.

"Better do as he says!" yelled Alfie, stepping out of Robin's line of sight. The portal fizzed and crackled open.

"Take your best shot," giggled the sprite. He put one foot through the portal, dragging Madeleine with him.

Robin released the arrow, shooting high. As it whistled over Alfie's head he saw that the tip was bulbous. The sprite, surprised that Robin had dared to shoot, grinned as the arrow thudded into the tree above him.

"Missed—" his jeer turned into a scream as a dark grey powder rained down from the broken arrowhead. He brushed frantically at his face, which looked as though it had been scalded, shaking his hands as the powder burnt them too. Alfie couldn't figure out what was happening. The powder had also showered Madeleine, but she seemed completely unharmed. She seized the opportunity to wrench herself free, and then grabbed the talisman. The sprite tried to catch her but Robin whistled to catch his attention and sent another arrow whizzing towards him.

"You'll regret that," the sprite screamed, leaping into the air as the arrow exploded on the cobbles by his bare feet. He dived towards the portal. "You'll wish you'd let me have the lens when *she* comes through." With that, he disappeared into the bright blue pool of light, which remained open behind him.

"Into the castle!" shouted Alfie as Robin and Amy grabbed Madeleine.

Alfie raced across the courtyard and snatched up Galileo from where he was cowering behind a large stone planter. The cat's fur was bristling as he snarled at the portal. A wind was starting to pick up, blowing a cool mist into the courtyard. Another of the ravens swept away over the walls. Galileo growled and clung tightly to Alfie's tunic as he ran back to the castle. Alfie looked over his shoulder and saw the source of the mist. It was swirling out from the tree.

"Close the doors!" he yelled as he ran into the castle. Amy and Robin swung the castle doors shut and bolted them. Galileo shot off up the stairs the second he was released.

Alfie grabbed the receiver from the phone in the hall and tried to remember how to call Muninn and Bone's offices. Glancing at the symbols on the strange old phone, he dialled the star and moon then tapped his fingers frantically on his leg as it rang and rang. It was nearly midnight, would anyone even be there? Robin was looking out through the hatch in the door watching the mist pouring from the tree.

At long last there was a click at the other end of the line and Emily's voice crackled out of the receiver. "Muninn and Bone's offices. Emily Fort—"

"Emily!" shouted Alfie. "Something's happening. Ashford wasn't Ashford. He tried to take the lens. He opened the portal; there's mist coming through!" The line was crackling so much that Alfie couldn't make out Emily's reply. "Emily!" He shouted over the noise, "Can you hear me?" More crackling. "Tell Caspian the portal is open!" With that the noise fizzled down to a soft hiss. The line was dead.

"You'd better see this, Alfie," said Robin. "Something's happening."

Alfie dropped the receiver and joined Robin on tiptoe at the hatch. The portal was starting to swirl again.

"Something's coming through." The words had barely left Alfie's lips when the fierce-looking elf that had led the raid on the castle stepped through. He was dragging something with him – a man. He tossed the wretched figure to the ground.

"Ashford!" screamed Alfie. Amy and Madeleine rushed to help unbolt the entrance. The butler looked up as they swung open the door, his face was drawn and bruised.

"Get back inside!" he cried. "Lock the doors and don't open them . . . no matter what!" The final raven circling the courtyard cawed and shot up into the last patch of clear sky as mist closed over it, sealing off the castle.

"Quiet." The elf shoved Ashford with his foot, as though he were a toy he was growing bored of.

"No!" shouted Alfie as Robin and Amy grabbed his arms. "We've got to help him!" The elf smiled and began to walk towards them. More elves spilled from the tree behind him as Alfie was dragged backwards into the castle

"Maddie, hit the switch!" shouted Robin, slamming the door and bolting it tight.

"Stop!" cried Alfie. "Ashford's still out there." Pale faced, Madeleine looked from Alfie to Amy and Robin who were pushing their backs to the door as the elves began to pound the other side.

"Sorry, Alfie." She flicked the security switch. Alfie heard the internal bolts sliding into place and the heavy crossbar dropped down across the huge doors, securing them fast. Iron grates rattled down in front of the stained glass windows and the torches on the walls flared to life as the castle barricaded them in.

Alfie turned on the others. "Why did you do that?" he shouted "You left him out there! With *them*!"

"There's nothing we can do right now," said Robin, nervously putting his hand on Alfie's shoulder. "Calm down. You saw the ravens leave. I bet they went to tell Caspian what happened. He'll send help."

Alfie pulled away from Robin, not wanting to admit that his cousin might be right. He couldn't bear it. Ashford was trapped on the other side of the castle doors and there was nothing he could do to help him.

"We should call Dad," said Madeleine, her voice still croaky from the pressure the sprite had put on her throat. "He's got his phone with him. We should warn them before they come up here."

"We can't," said Alfie, picking up the receiver. He clicked the hook down a few times but there was no dial tone, just faint eerie static that seemed filled with whispering voices.

"What's wrong?" asked Robin, "Did they cut the line?"

"There isn't a line to cut," said Alfie, passing him the phone. "But they've done something."

"What if it's the mist?" said Robin. "Maybe it's blocking the signals."

They all stared silently at the useless phone as the elves hammered on the doors.

"We could light the beacons at the top of the towers," said Madeleine, "Or flash an SOS with our torches."

"No one will see," said Alfie. "The mist has surrounded the whole castle."

"There must be *some* way of getting a message to our parents," said Robin.

"I know who we can ask," said Alfie.

Artan's roar of fury almost shook his tower when he heard about the return of the elves. All four of them had to hold on to his fur to stop him swooping down to the courtyard to take them on by himself.

"We need to get a message out," said Alfie. "Can you think of a way?"

"It's a message you need delivering, is it?" growled the bear. "Well I've got a message to deliver to *them*!"

"Artan, stop!" said Alfie, grabbing the bear again. "We need to send for help."

"Why?" asked Artan. "I could fly you all out of here right now!"

"No," said Robin immediately. "We don't know enough about that mist. It's blocking signals and we don't know what it might do to us. No one has come through it yet. Maybe they can't."

Alfie hadn't even thought about this, but Robin had a point.

"You know your problem?" said Artan. "You're alive! I'm not, so I can take your message. There isn't much that mist can do to harm me, is there?"

Alfie didn't like the idea, but with the elves camped out in the courtyard, Artan was their best hope.

"Are you sure about this?" he asked, flicking a switch to raise the security grate over Artan's tower window.

"Sure? I'm only sorry you won't let me take a crack at them myself! Now, what's the message?"

"Find a way to speak to Caspian. Tell him to send help, and to let Dad know we're OK." Alfie really wanted to get a message straight to his dad, but knew it wouldn't be the best time for him to meet Artan.

"You can rely on me."

"Thanks, Artan. Good luck."

The bear shot out of the window, punching a hole through the mist, which closed behind him.

"Come on," said Alfie. "Let's see what they're up to."

He led the way to the eastern tower and into the small armoury. He left the torches on the wall unlit in case the light alerted the elves. The two windows here were cross-shaped slits indented deep into the thick castle wall, too narrow for security grates to be necessary.

The four chain-mail tunics in the centre of the room seemed to make sense now.

"Do you think they were left for us?" asked Robin. "Maybe Orin somehow knew we would need them?"

"I don't think I want to know," said Alfie as he slid along the wall to one of the windows. He could make out roughly half of the courtyard through it.

"What are they doing?" asked Robin, silently

fighting Madeleine for a place at the other window. "Can you see Ashford?"

Several elves were pacing the courtyard, examining the grates over the windows while avoiding contact with the iron. A few had climbed up to the lower battlements and were trying to find a way into the castle. The rest had lit a fire and were sitting around it, checking their bows and the flights on their arrows. The tall leader paced among them, occasionally barking orders, which were instantly obeyed.

"They're looking around, but they don't seem in much of a rush to get in," said Alfie. "Maybe they're waiting for something?"

Ashford had been dragged over into the courtyard garden where he lay weakly against a stone bench. The blue light from the portal mingled with the flickering flames, giving the whole scene an unearthly appearance.

Suddenly all of the elves looked up into the misty sky above them.

"What are they looking at, Alfie?" said Madeleine. "I can't see from this side."

Alfie hardly needed to look at the shadow in the sky to know what it was. "Come on, Artan," he muttered under his breath as the shape darted in and out of the mist. "Get out of here!"

"Why is he flying in circles, Al?" asked Amy, pressing her head close to Alfie's to stare through the same horizontal slit. "Did you ask him to do that?"

"Of course not," said Alfie, watching Artan dart purposefully into the mist for a third time. "What is he up to?"

The elves had all leapt to their feet and several had nocked arrows to their bows. Their leader was holding his arm aloft, and he dropped it suddenly as the bear floated dazedly back out of the mist.

"*Artan!*" screamed Madeleine as the elves released their arrows. The leader immediately turned his gaze to the window and another flurry of arrows bounced off the stonework. One made it through the narrow opening to thud into the wooden rafters.

"Away from the windows," shouted Alfie. They all slammed their backs to the curved wall and edged along it towards the door.

"Did they hit him?" whispered Madeleine as she inched along by Alfie's side. Alfie wished he knew.

"I don't know. He flew towards his tower. We need to go and see if he's—"

Alfie was cut off by a cold voice shouting up from the courtyard.

"I am Merioch, the Queen's lieutenant. We have your servant, and you have something of ours. The solution is obvious."

"Alfie, get back here," called Robin as Alfie darted back to crouch by the window. He could see Ashford kneeling by the tall figure who was holding him up by his stained shirt. He barely looked conscious.

"Leave him alone!" Alfie yelled.

"Hand over the lens and he is yours," called the elf. "Are you so cruel as to leave him with us when you could easily set him free?"

"We don't have it," called Alfie. "Your spy took it when he opened the portal."

Merioch let go of Ashford and the butler slumped to the ground. "Lies," he spat. "The Queen's pet might be a trickster, but he is loyal." He put his foot on Ashford's injured shoulder and pushed down. The butler let out a ragged cry of pain. "STOP!" screamed Madeleine, shaking off Robin's grip and rushing over to join Alfie. "You're going to be *so* sorry you did that!"

Merioch ignored her and pointed up at Alfie. "The Queen will arrive tomorrow. If we do not have the lens by then, we will take the castle, and everything in it."

Alfie fought to think up some threat that might make the elves give up Ashford, but Amy grabbed his arm and dragged him from the room together with a furiously flailing Madeleine who was being pulled along by Robin.

"We've got to help him," said Alfie, as Robin closed the door to the tower.

"I know," said Amy. "We will. But first we need to check on Artan."

Panting his way up the spiral stairs, Alfie could hear a groaning and a flapping noise coming from Artan's room. A cold dread gripped his stomach as he entered. Artan was flopping around on the floor, snapping his jaws at an arrow that was stuck halfway through his back. A second arrow lay next to him, snapped in two by the bear's jaws.

"Artan!" yelled Alfie, rushing to the bear and breaking the remaining arrow in two to remove it without causing any more damage. "Are you OK? Does it hurt?"

The bear raised his head weakly. "I feel as though I should be in heaven," he croaked.

"What do you mean?" cried Madeleine, grasping at the bear's paw. "You said you're not alive, so how can you be dying? Please don't leave us!"

"Let me guess," said Amy as Artan let out a

long wheeze. She stuck her finger through one of the holes in his fur. "You're feeling holey, aren't you?"

Artan seemed to recover immediately and flew up into the air so that the flaming torch on the wall shone through the two holes in his fur. "That's right!" he guffawed.

"Seriously?" cried Alfie. "Puns? At a time like this. You still can't help yourself! What happened to you out there? You didn't seem to know what you were doing."

The bear floated down a little sheepishly.

"I didn't. Well, not all the time. I knew I had to get help, but as soon as I flew into the mist, I forgot what I was doing and where I was going. I kept finding myself heading back to the castle, and then I'd remember I was supposed to be getting help. It happened every time I tried to leave."

Madeleine pulled the bear across her lap and touched one of the holes in his fur. "Does it hurt?" she asked.

"Not one bit. But it might make our flights a little breezy!"

"I think I can help," said Madeleine. "I've got a sewing kit in my bag. I'll get you fixed up."

"*You've* got a *sewing* kit?" asked Alfie, as if she'd

just told him the sky was green. "And you know how to use it?"

"Mum said she won't buy me a new quiver if I ruin any more clothes, so I've been patching up holes for months." She patted Artan's fur. "I'll have you looking as handsome as ever in no time."

"This mist," said Robin. "There's no way through it."

Alfie looked out of Artan's window. The mist was rolling around on all sides of the castle about twenty metres beyond the walls. He felt as if they were under a white dome. The more he stared into it, the harder it was to believe the world still existed beyond the grey wall.

"There's got to be something we can do," said Madeleine, jumping to her feet. "Couldn't Orin's magic blast a hole in it the way it blasted Murkle and Snitch?"

"It didn't blast them," said Alfie. "It fed on their change magic."

"So feed it on the mist then!"

"It doesn't work like that."

"How do you know? You haven't even tried."

"Calm down, Maddie," said Robin impatiently.

"Don't you dare tell me to calm down," she shouted. "At least I'm trying to think of something!"

"Maddie, it won't work because the magic feeds on energy or life," said Alfie. "This mist, it seems . . . dead."

"He's right," said Amy.

"So we're just supposed to sit here until someone rescues us? Like . . . like fairy-tale princesses?" Madeleine slumped down into a chair and picked angrily at the embroidered armrests, completely removing a small hummingbird.

"Maybe that's the *best*-case scenario," said Amy softly. "If nothing can get out, I bet nothing can get in either."

"So there's no one to help us?" said Madeleine.

The thought had run through Alfie's head and he had already reached the same terrible conclusion: they were on their own.

9

A Daring Rescue

Alfie and Robin changed out of their Beltane tunics and into ordinary clothes in Alfie's bedroom. The realization they were trapped, with no hope of rescue, had cast a grim silence over everyone.

They headed to Amy's room where she was pinching together the sides of a hole in Artan's back. Madeleine was expertly stitching it together, grimacing as she tugged the long needle through the tough leather of the bear's hide.

"Done," she said at last, snipping the nylon thread and patting the bear's fur back into place as Artan twisted his neck around to admire her handiwork. Alfie couldn't even see where the hole had been.

"You're a fine surgeon, lassie," Artan commented. Madeleine managed only the tiniest of smiles.

"I've been thinking," said Alfie. "If no one is coming for us, we need to get Ashford away from *them*, and we need to do it quickly."

"I'll help," said Artan immediately. "I can swoop down and grab him."

"The elves are all around him," said Robin. "You wouldn't be able to get in and out quickly enough."

"We could create a distraction," said Amy. "It would need to be a big one though."

"What if we split up and throw things down at them from the battlements and the towers?" suggested Madeleine.

"Too dangerous," said Alfie. "You've seen how quick they are with their arrows." He thought hard. *What could distract the elves long enough for Artan to rescue Ashford, without putting everyone in danger?*

"Robin. Those arrows you shot at the sprite. Do you have any more?"

Robin pulled two from his quiver. "There are more in your dad's workshop."

Alfie took one of the arrows. It was quite heavy and had a roughly cast bulbous metal tip. He shook it. Something that sounded like sand was packed inside the tip. He remembered the sprite's reaction when the arrow had exploded over him and suddenly realized what Robin had done.

"You filled them with iron filings?" he laughed.

Robin grinned.

"You're a genius! So *that's* what you and Dad were making. OK – Maddie, Robin, I'm going to need you two to create a distraction by shooting from the windows in the armoury. They're not going to like these at all!"

"I'm not sure how well I'll be able to shoot," said Madeleine, weighing an arrow in her hand. "These are really unbalanced!"

"You managed fine firing those wadded arrows at the wicker man yesterday," said Robin. "And we won't need to be too accurate." He fitted one of the arrows to the bow Alfie had given him. "Just hit a hard surface near them. When the arrowhead breaks, the iron will do all the work. Come on, help me grab the rest."

As well as the arrows, there was a smaller crate in the workshop filled with metal balls. Each was a little bigger than a ping-pong ball and sealed with a small cork stopper. They made the same swishing noise as the arrows when Alfie shook them.

"Careful. They're fragile," said Robin, loading them into his backpack while Madeleine filled their quivers with arrows.

"Keep away from the windows," said Alfie as they headed back into the little armoury. "OK, here's the plan. While Maddie and Robin cause a distraction with the arrows, I'll be behind the upper battlements waiting for the right moment to send Artan down. Artan, you'll need to leave from your room so they don't see you coming. There's a gap between the outer walls and the mist. Fly down and float just outside the courtyard walls. I'll give a blast on your whistle when it's time for you to go in. You've got to be quick. Then grab Ashford and take him straight back to your tower."

The bear bobbed his head and gave a little salute.

"What about me?" asked Amy.

"I need you to go with Artan to his tower and wait there to help Ashford when he gets back."

Amy looked a little reluctant to miss the action but didn't argue.

"You be careful out there, Al," she said as she hopped on to Artan's back.

"Take these," said Robin, reaching into his backpack and offering Alfie and Amy a walkie-talkie each. "I've got three. They still work; I think it's because they're all within the mist dome."

"Let us know when Artan is in place," said Alfie. "And when he gets back with Ashford."

"Will do." Amy clipped the device to her belt.

"Ready, m'lady?" said Artan.

"Yup, let's go."

As Artan zoomed away through the castle towards his tower, Alfie heard Amy's distant voice add, "And don't ever call me lady!"

Alfie swallowed hard as he looked up and spotted the arrow Merioch had shot through the window and into the rafters. He took a chain-mail tunic from one of the wooden mannequins. "We should put these on," he told the twins. "The windows are tiny, but the elves are *really* good shots."

"Hmph. So are we!" said Madeleine, strapping on an archer's leather wristguard she had found with the armour.

As they finished pulling on the chain mail, the radio crackled to life.

Amy's voice came through the walkie-talkie as Alfie picked it up. "Ready when you are."

"Stand by," said Alfie. "Ready?" he asked the twins. They both gave him the thumbs up as he silently unlocked the door that led outside.

"Take these with you, Alfie." Robin handed over his backpack containing the small metal balls. "Iron bombs. For emergencies."

Alfie took the backpack and crawled out on to the battlements, keeping to a low crouch to remain hidden. About halfway across, he raised his head to peek through one of the gaps. The elves were back around the fire and didn't seem to be acting with any kind of urgency since their ultimatum. Had they just assumed Alfie would give in? He couldn't wait to show them otherwise.

Ashford was sitting against one of the fruit trees in the courtyard garden. He seemed too weak to move. The two elves guarding him were paying more attention to a game that involved something that looked like small bleached animal bones than they were to their prisoner.

Alfie turned to the armoury where he could see Madeleine in position at her window. He gave her the OK sign with his fingers. She nodded and released the first arrow.

A piercing screech echoed up from the courtyard, followed by angry cries and scrabbling noises. Crouching close to the floor, Alfie noticed a drainage hole in the stonework and lay down to look through it. The elves were falling over each other to grab their bows and arrows. Several were leaping around brushing the filings off their skin and out of their hair. Three of them raised their bows to point at where Madeleine and Robin were shooting from, but they were too slow. Two more arrows smashed into the wall beside them, the tips exploding into a shower of black dust. The elves dropped their bows and flapped at themselves as if they had caught fire.

Alfie smiled grimly to see the small army in complete disarray as the twins kept the arrows flying. *That'll teach you to invade my castle*, he thought to himself. The elves guarding Ashford finally left his side to help the others. Alfie raised the silver whistle to his lips and blew a silent blast on it. A dark shadow swooped over the far wall and down to where Ashford lay.

Alfie held his breath as Artan nudged the butler with his nose. He seemed barely conscious.

"Come on, Ashford," Alfie whispered, willing him to move before the twins ran out of arrows. Finally Ashford roused himself enough to shuffle on to the bear's back. Artan tried to take off but the butler slid from his back, unable to hold on with his hands tied. Alfie's heart was in his mouth as the bear gnawed the ropes that bound Ashford's hands. The elves were hiding behind trees, planters and stone benches, and still hadn't noticed Artan freeing their captive. None of them seemed to want to risk being caught in the iron rain. There was no sign of their leader, Merioch, and without him the others seemed unable to take control of the situation.

Ashford's bonds fell away. As he began to pull himself back on to Artan's back there was a flash of blue from the oak. Merioch stepped out of the portal, his cold eyes immediately assessing the scene. He darted around the tree as an arrow hit the spot where he had been standing.

"Fools! Look to your prisoner!" he shouted as Artan rose carefully into the air. Ashford was holding on tightly with his one good arm.

"Bring him down!" The elves dashed out of hiding, seemingly more scared of their leader than showers of searing iron.

Artan was moving as fast as he could, but it wasn't quick enough. He had to keep Ashford from falling. Alfie looked to Madeleine. She pointed to her empty quiver. "We're all out," she mouthed.

The elves raised their bows against Artan. An idea hit Alfie as he noticed their backs were to the fire. Reaching into Robin's backpack he grabbed some of the iron bombs and hurled them down into the courtyard. Two missed, but four landed in the fire, exploding spectacularly. The flames roared up like a gigantic sparkler, spitting masses of flaming sparks at the shrieking elves. Alfie could hardly believe the chaos he had caused. He watched delightedly as Artan whizzed up over the castle's rooftops with Ashford safely on board.

Undaunted by the flames and stinging iron, Merioch rolled away from the fire to grab his bow. Alfie was suddenly very aware that his head was completely visible. He dropped to the floor as an arrow whistled through the battlements. The elf continued to fire arrow after arrow in rapid succession. They bounced off the stonework, clattering down around Alfie as he crawled back into the tower on his elbows. Madeleine and Robin had pulled back from their posts at the windows. They rushed over to slam the door behind him, bolting it shut as arrows thudded into the woodwork on the other side.

The radio crackled again.

"We got him!" Amy shouted, so loudly that Alfie almost dropped the receiver. The twins let out a loud cheer then dived to the ground as an arrow flew through the tiny window slit, scraping

Madeleine's chain mail as it passed between them.

"Let's get out of here!" said Alfie, as more arrows clattered off the castle wall just outside the windows.

As they hurried down the corridor to Artan's tower, the tapestry that covered the entrance swept aside. Amy held it back as Artan floated carefully through the doorway carrying Ashford, his head resting on the bear's as if it were a pillow. His eyes were open and he smiled weakly to see Alfie and the twins by his side.

"Ashford, it's really you," cried Alfie. He clasped the butler's good arm, trying to hide his shock at his haggard appearance. Ashford's usually beaming face was drawn and bruised, his eyes bloodshot and ringed with dark circles. "Artan, bring him to my room. He can use my bed."

Ashford groaned as Artan carefully landed on Alfie's huge four-poster bed. Alfie and Amy helped to slide him off the bear and propped him up against the pillows.

"It's good to be home," he croaked in an attempt at cheeriness as Amy and the twins fussed around him.

"How badly hurt are you?" asked Alfie, his eyes dropping to the stained bandages wrapped poorly around Ashford's shoulder under his torn shirt.

"I'll live," said Ashford, wincing as Amy and Robin helped him off with his tattered shirt and began to unwrap the bandages. "But my wellbeing wasn't exactly their top priority. They— Argh!" he cried out as the last of the bandages was peeled away from his shoulder. Alfie fought the urge to turn away at the sight and sickly smell of the dark wound.

"That doesn't look good," said Amy, glancing at Alfie as Ashford closed his eyes and winced in pain. "He needs a doctor."

Alfie looked around helplessly and spotted a little pot on his bedside table. He grabbed it. "This is the last of the ointment that the doctors put on us at Muninn and Bone. Maybe it will help?"

"We need to clean him up first," said Madeleine, taking charge. "Have you got a first aid kit, and a bottle of iodine? That's what Granny uses on my cuts. It stings, but they never get infected."

"I don't know," said Alfie, "Maybe in the kitchen?"

"I'll take a look," said Amy, hurrying away, as though glad of something to do.

"I'll get some hot water and bandages," said Robin, following her.

Alfie was tempted to follow them to avoid looking at the damage to Ashford's shoulder, but the butler's eyes were open again.

"Alfie," he said weakly. "I'm so sorry."

"What for?" asked Alfie, focusing on Ashford's gaunt face and trying not to let his eyes slip to the wound, which Madeleine was examining without the slightest revulsion. He was amazed at how little blood seemed to bother her – even Amy had rushed from the room as soon as she could.

"It's my fault they're here." The butler's voice cracked slightly as he spoke. "I used the portal, twice. I was so careful about it, but they discovered I had been through and the second time they tracked and followed me. I've been a fool."

"But you're the one that's hurt," said Alfie. "We're fine. They can't get in, and they can't keep that mist around for ever, can they? Someone will come for us, eventually."

"You don't understand what I've done." Ashford grabbed Alfie's arm. "They didn't know the lens was here. When they took me I told them it was in Muninn and Bone's vaults where they couldn't reach it."

"So why are they here then?" asked Madeleine, pausing in her examination.

"It wasn't deliberate," said Ashford, his grip on Alfie tightening. "You've got to know that."

Alfie stared back into Ashford's pained eyes. "You told them?"

"Yes," Ashford's voice broke. "They drugged me, and their sprites took on familiar forms so that I hardly knew who I was speaking to: you, Caspian, Emily. When I finally came back into myself, they knew about the talisman and the fact that it was here. I had told them. They had left a sprite on this side in the form of a mouse in case he could find out anything else, but they were sure that it was with Caspian until I told them otherwise, and then they gathered for when the sprite reopened the portal at Beltane. It's all my fault."

Ashford seemed unable to meet Alfie's eyes.

"Even if you hadn't told them," Alfie said at last, "they would have found out anyway. The sprite they left on this side disguised himself as you. He saw me wearing the talisman and stole it to open up the portal. He would have taken it through if Madeleine hadn't snatched it away from him."

"You see?" said Madeleine. "It didn't matter that you told them."

"But I led them through in the first place!" exploded Ashford. "You don't know Merioch. He's biding his time until the Queen gets here, then nothing will keep them out."

"That's enough!" snapped Madeleine, sounding very much like Granny. "We're safe for the moment. Let's not waste time worrying about who's to blame and what *might* happen."

"She's right," said Alfie. "Come on, we'll fix you up, and then figure out a way out of this."

Robin and Amy reappeared with a large first aid kit and a bowl full of water that smelt like antiseptic. Ashford sank back into Alfie's pillows, his expression a mixture of guilt and relief as Madeleine went to work on his wounds.

10

Under the Dome

Alfie's watch told him it was long after midnight. The powerlessness he felt at the situation his talisman had landed them in grew worse as he watched the twins patching up Ashford. The butler looked as though he hadn't eaten in days. Desperate to feel useful, Alfie headed down to the undercroft pantry with Amy to find some food. Galileo followed to check whether there were any mice hiding down there.

"Ash doesn't look good," said Amy as they raided the pantry. It was upside down after being ransacked by the fake Ashford in his search for the lens.

"I know," said Alfie, digging out cheeses, chutney and pâté from the jumble of food on the shelves. He had been thinking the same. Ashford's wound had gone so long without treatment that it must be infected. Madeleine was doing her best with the salve Emily had given them, but Ashford needed a real doctor. "We've got to find a way out."

"It would take a while, but what if we dig under the dome?" said Amy. "Artan could fly us down between the courtyard walls and the mist. They wouldn't see us, and as long as we're quiet, they'd never know we were digging our way out."

Alfie stared at her. "You're right. I don't know how far the mist extends, but if we all work together we'll get out eventually. We've even got enough shovels for the four of us in. . ." he paused.

"They're in the shed, aren't they?" said Amy. "The one in the courtyard?"

Alfie sighed. "Well, we nearly had a plan." He passed her a loaf of bread and gathered up the rest of the food.

"Come on, Leo," he said to the cat as it scratched the door to the cellars. "There's nothing for you down there." Galileo obediently bounded up the stairs to the kitchen in anticipation of being fed. As Alfie followed, he was hit with a sudden thought.

Perhaps there was another way under the mist after all. He dropped the food back on to the shelf and unlocked the door Galileo had been scratching at.

"Where are we going?" Amy asked.

"Out."

Alfie grabbed one of the flaming torches from the wall and led the way through the cellars, pausing briefly to grab a very long coil of rope from one of the rooms on the way. Amy hurried after him as he unlocked a large studded door and followed the stairs down into the cellars below.

Their footsteps echoed in the dark labyrinth as Alfie headed for the central chamber and the strange round pool it held. He had leapt into it once to save Robin, and a strong current had dragged them both out into Lake Archelon. They had nearly drowned that night.

"Give me a hand with this," he said as they reached the pool. His dad had covered it up with a large wooden lid to prevent any further accidents. With Amy's help, Alfie slid it aside.

"We're going out through there?" asked Amy, the dark water reflecting the flickering flames of the torch.

"We've got to try something," said Alfie. He tied one end of the rope to a metal ring on the wall.

"There's a strong current on the way down, so I'll need to use this to pull myself back up after you get out."

"Wait, you want me to go – leaving you all here?"

"One of us needs to stay and let the others know, and you're the best swimmer by miles. If anyone can get out under the mist, it's you."

"So you just expect me to clear off and leave you all here?" said Amy sharply. "You think I'd do that?"

Alfie sighed. "It's not about being brave enough to stay. We need you to tell Dad and Caspian what's happening in here. Maybe we can all swim out under the mist, but we'd need lots of help to get Ashford out that way."

Amy seemed slightly mollified, but Alfie knew she couldn't bear the thought of leaving them.

"OK. Let's get this done then." She took off her shoes and socks and stripped down to her T-shirt. "I'm leaving my trousers on," she said firmly as she stood waiting for Alfie.

"Me too," said Alfie, glad that he could stop trying to remember which pair of underpants he was wearing. He slipped off his chain mail, unclipped his walkie-talkie and tied the loose end of the rope through his trouser loops, knotting it tightly.

Alfie's breath caught in his throat as they lowered themselves into the freezing-cold water. The strong current of the water flowing beneath the castle dragged at his feet.

"Hold tight to the side," he warned through chattering teeth. "When we let go, we'll be sucked down and into another tunnel. There's a metal grate at the end with a big hole in it. Squeeze through into the lake and we'll meet at the surface. OK, ready?"

They both took a deep breath and submerged, letting the current pull them down and along. The last time Alfie had done this he had been tumbling after Robin in a blind panic. This time he managed to stay fairly calm, despite the freezing-cold water chilling him to the bone. Amy swam ahead as though she did this sort of thing every day, and had already slipped gracefully through the grate by the time he reached it. He eased himself through, trying to avoid the sharp edges, then kicked off towards the surface of the lake, breaking through a few feet from Amy, who was gazing into the veil of mist.

"I didn't think this through," said Alfie, shivering as he treaded water by her side. "It's pitch-black underwater. We're not going to be able to see if the mist goes right the way down."

"Yeah, I realized on the way up," said Amy. "It'd be risky to swim too deep, but we might be able to see if it goes down below the surface. Come on, let's take a closer look."

Alfie swam after Amy, very glad he had thought to bring the rope. There was no way they would find their way back through the inky water to the grate without it.

They stopped at the edge of the mist and bobbed there for a while.

"It sounds weird, doesn't it?" he said.

"What do you mean? I don't hear anything."

"Exactly. It's like its sucking in and blocking out all other noises. Like we're wearing earplugs or something." Alfie even felt as though the mist was trying to mute the words coming out of his mouth.

"OK, I'm going under." Amy took a few deep breaths, and then disappeared below the surface. Alfie counted under his breath as he waited for her to reappear. Faint laughter filtered down from the castle courtyard far above, followed by drums and the start of a song in Elvish. By the sound of the unpleasant laughter that punctuated the verses, he was glad he didn't understand what they were singing about.

His count reached eighty-five seconds. Just as he was starting to worry, Amy broke the surface. She wiggled her finger in one ear to clear the water and shook her head. "It's no good. I can only see for a couple of metres, but it looks like it goes all the way down and all the way around."

Alfie's heart sank. He had been so sure he had found a way to outwit the elves. As the water chilled him to the bone, he regretted acting so hastily. Robin would have seen the flaws in the plan before they even set foot in the water. Laughter rang out again and Alfie felt sudden fury at their helplessness. He needed to do something. He swam a couple of strokes towards the mist but the rope around his waist pulled tight. He began to loosen it.

"Wait!" cried Amy. "What are you doing?"

"Take this," said Alfie, handing her the rope. "I'm going through it."

Amy grabbed his arm before he could swim a stroke. "Are you crazy? You saw what happened when Artan tried. It made him forget what he was trying to do."

"I know. But, Artan is a bear. A very clever bear,

but maybe a human wouldn't be confused the way he was."

"Alfie, don't!" hissed Amy, but Alfie swam out of reach leaving her holding the rope back to the castle. "Don't be an idiot!"

"I've *got* to try," said Alfie. "I'm just going to swim a little way in to see what it does." Before Amy could say another word, he swam into the mist.

It was as though someone had pressed a mute button on the world. Surrounded by the white-grey mist, Alfie felt as though he was floating in some kind of limbo. He began to swim. A hint of a whisper brushed by his left ear. He stopped and turned around but there was no one there. Another whisper from his right. He paddled around in a circle, but all he could hear was his own splashing in the silence. He was alone.

Focus, Alfie, he told himself. But what was it he had to focus on? Was he supposed to be going somewhere? It was so pleasant here in the mist he hardly wanted to leave. But he *had* to. He had to find someone – who?

"Alfie!" a voice was calling his name. A distant muffled voice quite unlike the whispers. "Alfie!" It was Amy. Maybe it was her he was trying to find. He tried to swim towards the voice, but couldn't quite figure out where it was coming from. "ALFIE!" Perhaps it was coming from beneath him. He stopped paddling and let himself float face down on the surface, his eyes open to search for Amy. It looked nice down there in the deep. Dark. Peaceful. He still couldn't see Amy. He decided to let himself sink down to look for her. He began to blow out bubbles of air, enjoying the tickling sensation as they brushed against his cheek. He felt himself begin to sink gently as the air left his lungs.

There was a sudden pain in the back of his head and he stopped sinking. Someone caught him by the hair and dragged his head up above the surface. "No, I've got to find Amy!" he spluttered.

"Shut up, idiot!" growled a voice close to his ear. *Amy?* Seconds later he was out of the mist and bobbing in the clear water where they had first emerged. The fuzziness that filled his head was clearing as everything became glaringly clear. He had failed.

"Follow me," hissed Amy, swimming towards the cliff face that dropped down from the castle. Alfie swam after her, following the cliff around until they were out of sight of the courtyard walls.

"Did I make it far?" asked Alfie, between chattering teeth.

"Far? You only got a couple of metres in before you started swimming in circles and trying to drown yourself. Luckily I was able to grab you from the edge when you got close enough, but even there I could feel it starting to affect me."

"So, there's really no way anyone is getting in or out," said Alfie, his heart sinking into his stomach as he stared out at the dome. This was happening because of his inheritance. He felt the weight of that fact like an anvil tied to his feet, dragging him down. "It's up to us."

He turned and began to paddle in the direction of the underwater entrance. "Come on, let's get back inside. Ashford might have a better idea."

Amy grabbed his arm.

"Alfie, we can't go back." Her face was pale in the moonlight as she held up her empty hands. Alfie stared at her and finally realized what she was telling him. The rope. It had gone.

"It wasn't long enough. I had to let it go when I swam over to get you. It sank."

Alfie stared. He couldn't blame Amy. He would have drowned if she hadn't come after him, but if they couldn't get back into the castle the others would think that the elves had taken them – they might even surrender. He had to get back inside, but without the rope there was no way to find the grate and swim against the current that flowed through the tunnel under the castle.

He looked up at the castle high atop the cliff. He could see the window to Artan's room.

"We could try climbing up there," said Amy, following his gaze.

Alfie had visited a climbing wall many times with Amy when he had lived in the city. The cliff was craggy and didn't look too difficult to climb, but the smoother castle stonework was a different story.

"Impossible." He shivered. His hands and arms were starting to feel numb.

"So we just hang around down here?"

"Unless you want to climb the hill and shout over the walls for them to lower the drawbridge. . ."

Amy slapped her hand over his mouth. "Move," she whispered urgently before swimming swiftly towards the cliff. Alfie followed. They pulled themselves up on to the rocks near the base of one of the narrow waterfalls that cascaded down from the castle moat and crawled quickly into a hollow behind it.

Amy pointed out at the lake as Alfie wedged himself into the hollow with her. He strained his eyes to see what had startled her. Something dark was skimming across the surface of the lake.

"What is it?" mouthed Amy.

It was difficult to make out the shape in the dark as they peered through a gap in the flowing water. Whatever it was, it seemed to be criss-crossing the lake, searching for something.

"Do you think they sent it? Do they know we're out here?"

"Maybe," whispered Alfie, but as the shape did a little flip before circling around again, Alfie's heart leapt. He let out a low whistle.

"What are you doing?" whispered Amy, slapping her hand over his mouth again. But she was too late; it turned and shot towards them. Alfie felt her grip on his wrist relax as she finally recognized the looming creature.

"Artan!" she cried as the bear splashed through the cascading water to join them in the little hollow.

"Funny time to go swimming," he boomed as he shook himself, showering them with water.

*

"How about we all stick together and not enact any daring missions without talking to each other first?" said Ashford.

"Agreed," said Alfie. He was sitting next to Amy in front of a blazing fire Robin had lit in the Great Hall fireplace. They were both still shivering, despite being back in their dry clothes.

Ashford was sitting rather stiffly in one of the armchairs, Madeleine cross-legged by his feet, keeping an eye on him as she stroked Galileo, who had stretched out in front of the fire as though he didn't have a care in the world.

"You're lucky we found Galileo yowling in the undercroft," said Robin. "He was scratching at the door to the cellars. When we realized you'd gone through there we figured out what you were trying to do. I hung around the pool for a bit, and when you didn't come back up we sent Artan to search for you."

"Thanks, Rob," said Alfie. He patted Artan's head, which was resting on the bench next to him.

"Next time you do something daft, take my whistle with you!" said the bear.

"I take it you didn't find a way out?" asked Madeleine.

"We couldn't get through the mist," said Alfie.

"It kind of dulls your brain the second you enter it. It makes you imagine things."

"The mists of forgetfulness," said Ashford. "Which I *could* have told you about *if* you'd spoken to me before heading off on your own. They border the elven realm. The elves can harness them, to an extent. You're lucky you didn't get far. Even if you had managed to journey through it – an almost impossible task – you would have come out the other side unable to remember even your own name."

Alfie shuddered despite the warmth of the fire.

Robin had collected up the food Alfie and Amy had left in the cellars and laid it out on the huge oak table. Ashford stayed in the armchair as they went over to eat.

"Are you sure you don't want anything?" asked Amy, pouring out glasses of apple juice. Ashford didn't answer. He was already asleep, lying against the wing of the chair.

"Is he going to be OK?" Alfie quietly asked Madeleine as he idly crumbled the crackers on his plate.

"I did the best I could with the wound," said Madeleine. "The salve seemed to help, but..." she turned to make sure Ashford was still asleep.

"It's bad. He's covered in bruises. I think he has a couple of broken ribs and maybe blood poisoning. He needs help. Soon."

They finished their meal in near silence, sharing worried glances every time Ashford made the slightest noise in his sleep. As the clock ticked past four o'clock, no one had come up with an even slightly workable escape plan. Alfie was fighting to stay awake and Madeleine's yawning was infectious.

"Maybe we should catch a few hours sleep," suggested Robin.

"I guess there's nothing else we can do," Alfie sighed.

They grabbed cushions from the Abernathy Room and made makeshift beds on the rugs in front of the fire. No one wanted to be alone.

Alfie lay awake long after Amy and his cousins had joined Ashford in sleep. He couldn't stop thinking about the elves in the courtyard. They had invaded his home, hurt his friends, and cut him off from his family. As tiredness overcame even his worries, he promised himself one thing – they wouldn't get away with it.

11

The Siege of Hexbridge Castle

A loud trumpeting rang through even the shuttered windows, wrenching Alfie from dark dreams. They had slept well into the afternoon.

"It's *her*!" Ashford pulled himself to his feet, groaning with pain. "They won't wait any longer, not now that she's here. Quick, put your chain mail back on."

"But they can't get in. So we're still safe – aren't we?" asked Robin as they hurriedly pulled on the mail shirts they had discarded before going to sleep. Ashford's face answered the question.

"We need to see what she's doing," he said

quickly. "Alfie, have you ever found anything that looks like a black mirror?"

"Yes. Just the other day, how did you—"

"Get it for me please."

Running through the entrance hall and up the stairs to the library, Alfie could hear loud chanting creeping into the castle as the elves welcomed their Queen.

The mirror was where he had left it, in a hidden compartment in his four-poster bed. Clasping it to his chest as he hurried downstairs, he wondered how Ashford could possibly know of its existence. He stopped as a terrible thought slunk into his mind. What if Ashford *didn't* know? Could they have been fooled by the same trick twice? He slipped the mirror behind the bottom of a tapestry before heading back to the Great Hall.

"Do you have it?" Ashford asked eagerly as Alfie returned. Alfie sat down across the table from him.

"How did you know about the mirror?" he asked. A strange look passed fleetingly over the butler's face.

"That doesn't matter right now," he said quickly. "We need to see what they are doing out there. I need that mirror."

"And I suppose you want the talisman too, for safekeeping or something like that?"

"What's going on in your head, Alfie?" asked Madeleine. "I cleaned that wound on his shoulder. It's real."

"That doesn't mean he's really him though," said Alfie, watching Ashford for anything that would give him away as an imposter. "Maybe it's another sprite doing a better job of imitating him this time."

"Oh, come on, Alfie!" said Madeleine as the elves began their drumming again in the courtyard. "We need to know what's going on out there."

"It's OK, Maddie," said Ashford touching her arm gently as he gazed back at Alfie. "He's right to be wary. It would take too long to explain how I know about the mirror right now, so ask me some questions instead. Things that others wouldn't know."

Alfie thought quickly. "What happened in the cellars during the Christmas play?"

"Murkle and Snitch, your teachers, attempted to burn open the seal that Orin set above the place where dragons sleep," said Ashford without a moment of hesitation. "I stopped you from running straight towards them, but they had heard you. I became careless and was knocked unconscious. You had to deal with them yourself."

Ashford looked away from Alfie as he said this. He either felt guilty over it, or he was a very good actor.

"OK, he proved he's him. *Now* will you get the mirror?" said Madeleine.

"One more thing," said Alfie. Madeleine let out an exasperated cry. "Emily Fortune. What is she to you?" Ashford met his eyes again.

"Everything." Alfie could see the same look in Ashford's eyes as he had seen in Emily's when she talked about him. No one could ever fake that. He ran back and grabbed the mirror from its hiding place.

"Courtyard," said Alfie firmly. He placed the mirror on the table and everyone gathered around. The black surface flickered to life, revealing the formidable woman they had seen at Muninn and Bone standing on one of the stone benches in the courtyard garden. Merioch stood on her right as she addressed around forty elves kneeling before her.

"What do you think she said?" asked Amy as the elves jumped up, thumped their fists to their chests and held their bows aloft. Their cheers could be heard through the castle doors.

162

"I don't know," said Alfie as the elves parted to create a path for the Queen as she strode towards the castle. "But I don't think she was telling them to go home." Alfie picked up the mirror and they rushed to the entrance hall, listening for a pounding on the door.

"What is she doing?" asked Madeleine as the knock they all expected didn't come. She pulled at Alfie's arm so that she could look into the mirror.

"Let go, Maddie. I can't see."

"Tilt the mirror," said Ashford, "You can use it to look around, like an eye."

Alfie tilted the mirror around until he could see the Queen standing before the door, surrounded by elves nocking arrows to their bows. She raised her hands and placed one on each of the huge doors.

"Is she trying to push them open?"

"Wait, what's happening around her fingers?" said Robin.

Alfie stared hard at the tiny figure in the mirror. Something was happening to the wood around her hands. The door began to groan and creak in its frame. Shoots and leaves were beginning to sprout from the ancient dead wood. A leaf unfurled from the keyhole. More and more sprang from every crack as the wood came back to life.

163

"She's coming through!" said Ashford. "We need to hide. Now!"

"Where?" cried Madeleine, looking frantically around the hall. "The cellars?"

"They'd find us," said Ashford. Roots began to crawl from the base of the door, tearing up the mosaic floor tiles.

"Orin's study!" said Alfie, clutching the talisman around his neck. "We'll be safe there. They can't get in without this."

"Let's go," said Ashford. Crumbling mortar was beginning to trickle down from the arched doorway.

"We left our bows in your room," said Madeleine. "I'll grab them." She darted ahead as the front door shuddered and a branch sprouted upwards, splitting the wood almost from floor to ceiling.

"Alfie, Robin, come and help me!" Amy cried. Ashford had stumbled on the stairs. As Amy pulled him to his feet, Alfie could see that his face was sickly grey.

"You go ahead," said Robin as they managed to lift Ashford on to Artan's back. "I'll grab the rest of the iron bombs!"

Alfie had no time to argue as Robin ran towards the workshop.

"Be quick!" he yelled back, but he was drowned out by two stone blocks crashing to the floor. The wooden doors mutated and twisted upwards as the wood seemed to remember its original tree form, tearing bricks and mortar apart as it stretched out its branches. Alfie could see hands reaching through the gap as the trees began to part.

"Let's move!" growled Artan. Alfie and Amy hurried along beside him as he carried Ashford up the stairs and along the corridor to the library. The elves' shouts and cheers echoed up through the entrance hall as the opening grew.

"Where's Robin?" panted Madeleine as she joined them, bows and quivers bouncing on her shoulder.

"Grabbing more arrows," said Alfie, hurrying to the panelled wall and opening the secret door to Orin's study with his talisman.

Artan floated through first, closely followed by Galileo who had come barrelling after them when he heard the destruction in the hall.

"Maddie, come on," said Amy, pulling at her arm. Madeleine looked as though she wanted to rush downstairs to find Robin. The shouting from the hall was more excited now. "They must be nearly through – get in here."

Alfie helped Ashford slide from Artan's back and into Orin's armchair, then wrapped the blanket that hung over the back of the chair around him. Madeleine was still in the library, watching out for Robin.

Alfie grasped the mirror again and said, "Entrance Hall." His heart dropped as he saw the hall strewn with rubble. The ancient doors had become two great trees, their branches forming a perfect archway – an archway that the Queen now walked through triumphantly, followed by her small army.

"Maddie, we need to close the door," called Ashford weakly.

"Not without Robin. He'll be here any second."

"He won't, Maddie," said Alfie, holding out the mirror to show her a tiny Robin looking frantically around a room hung with tools. "See, he's still in the workshop; he can't get through the hall without them seeing him. We need to close the door." He hated saying it, but he knew Robin wouldn't want them to risk their safety for his.

Madeleine pulled back as Alfie took her arm and tried to drag her through the passageway. "We can't leave him," she cried.

"Maddie, we've got no choice—" Alfie stopped as

the walkie talkie he had clipped back on to his belt beeped loudly: Robin must still have his with him.

"Robin?" he said into the radio.

"Alfie, I'm stuck here," whispered Robin's voice. "Don't wait for me."

"Robin," cried Madeleine, snatching the radio from Alfie. "We're not closing the door until you get here."

"You've got to, Maddie," said Robin. "Don't worry about me. I've locked the door, and if they get in I've got somewhere to hide. Look in the mirror if you don't believe me."

Alfie held the black mirror out to Madeleine. Robin was waving as though not quite sure where they would be watching him from.

"See?" he said, lifting the top of the window seat to reveal a storage space. "I'll be OK."

Madeleine let out a choked sob. "Just stay hidden, Robin. We'll find a way to help you. I promise!"

Madeleine finally let Alfie pull her inside. The panel slid shut as the sounds of elves rampaging through the castle grew closer. Alfie gave Amy a nod and she swiftly closed the inner door, shutting them safely into the secret room.

*

They spent the next hour huddled together on the rug by Ashford's feet, watching the mirror. Alfie flinched at each loud noise as the elves rampaged through the castle, turning rooms upside down in their search for the talisman and the castle's occupants. It filled him with fury to watch them rummaging through his things. Polluting *his* home with their presence.

The battery on Robin's radio was running low, so they had agreed not to talk unless it was essential. Galileo was curled up on one of Orin's highest shelves, keeping his eyes firmly fixed on Artan who had come to rest on the back of the armchair where Ashford was sitting. After many months the cat seemed to have realized that Artan wasn't going to eat him, but this was the closest he had ever been to the dog-like bear and he wasn't taking any chances.

Sick of watching the elves, Alfie let Madeleine take the mirror to Orin's desk where she sat hunched over it, watching Robin like a hawk. He adjusted the blanket over Ashford. The butler seemed to be in a half faint. His skin was clammy and his face almost grey. Alfie was seriously worried about him. He lit a fire in the hearth and fanned the flames with an old set of bellows.

Amy removed her star-printed neck scarf and moistened it from a bottle of water she had managed to grab during the dash from the Great Hall. She dabbed Ashford's forehead with the damp cloth. Alfie fought the urge to tell her not to waste water, wondering how long the little bottle would have to last.

A crash from the library made them all jump and roused Ashford a little.

"It's OK," the butler whispered. "They won't find us in here."

Alfie silently fought Madeleine for the mirror as she watched a group of elves searching the ground floor, getting closer and closer to the room where Robin was hiding.

"Library," he whispered. Madeleine and Amy looked over his shoulders as the mirror revealed a fisheye view of the library. Five elves were creeping among the shelves, arrows nocked to their bows as they searched. Alfie held his breath as they reached the wall with the secret door, feet away from where they all sat in Orin's study. He clasped Artan's jaws to stop him from growling, but the elves were more interested in the fireplace, looking up the large chimney to see if anyone was hiding up there. Finally satisfied, they filed out of the library leaving one elf behind to stand guard. He stretched and settled into one of the cosy chairs near the fireplace, taking occasional swigs from a silver flask on his hip.

"What is *she* doing?" asked Ashford weakly. Alfie tried the Great Hall first. One of the grand carved chairs had been dragged from the head of the dining table to the centre of the room. The Queen sat regally on her new throne directing the elves in their search. She was wearing a delicate silver crown studded with several large gems.

"Get your hands off that," Alfie muttered under his breath as one of the elves found the silver sparrow on the table and brought it to the Queen. She wound it up and clapped her hands in delight as it flew around the room and returned to her. She tapped it on the top of its head and it sidled up her arm to sit on her shoulder, where it began to preen its wings.

"How did she do that?" asked Amy.

"The same way that she got through the front door," winced Ashford.

"You're saying she brought the bird to life?" said Alfie, eyes wide.

"Not exactly. But I doubt it will ever need to be wound again." The butler slumped forwards as though even speaking was too much for him.

Alfie eased him back into the chair and felt for his pulse. He wasn't sure what it should feel like, but it didn't seem strong. Amy poured some of the water into a little cup and held it to his lips. Ashford sipped weakly.

"Is there anything we can do for you?" she asked.

"There's only one person that can help me," said Ashford, wiping away the drops that had trickled down his chin. "The druid."

"You mean Orin?" said Alfie. "Caspian told us about you being able to timeslip too. Can you go back and get his help?"

Ashford shook his head weakly. "The pain is too distracting; I'm too weak to focus."

"Then teach me!" said Alfie. "I'll ask Orin for something to help you. Maybe he'll have a way to help us all."

"But you've only ever managed it by accident," said Ashford. "It took me months of practice to control the ability, and yours works differently to mine. What if it goes wrong?"

"Then I'm lucky I have you to guide me through it," said Alfie, fixing Ashford with a firm stare.

The butler smiled weakly. "I assume there's no point in arguing?"

Alfie shook his head.

"Then I'll try. But first, let me give you a message for Orin. Please, bring me some paper."

Alfie grabbed a blank notebook from Orin's desk where Madeleine was still huddled over the mirror.

"You can dictate to me, if you like?"

Ashford shook his head. "It's safer if you don't know what I am going to ask of him." He winced in pain as he began to write.

"They're trying to get into the workshop!" cried Madeleine suddenly. "They're going to find Robin." In the blackness of the mirror, three elves were throwing themselves against the workshop door. Madeleine changed the view to the workshop. Robin was climbing into the window seat. He reached up and made an OK sign for the benefit of anyone watching before lowering the lid.

Madeleine yelped as the door crashed open and elves spilled into the workshop. Alfie held his breath as he watched them stalk carefully around the iron tools, prodding the ticking and spinning devices that his dad had been working on. Two of them investigated the adjoining forge, while the other lingered near where Robin was hiding.

"They're going to find him!" said Madeleine, her fingers gripping Alfie's arm so tightly he had to grit his teeth to stop himself shouting out. The two that had searched the forge returned and nodded to the third who reluctantly sat down on the window seat as they left the room.

"They're leaving him on guard," said Amy. "Robin won't be able to leave."

"But he's got to get out!" cried Madeleine. "He'll run out of air!"

"He'll be OK for a few hours at least," said Ashford. "As long as he stays calm. And we know Robin is good at that."

"Maybe the guard won't stay that long," added Alfie. "I'm sure he'll be fine." But the thought of Robin cooped up in the stuffy box with one of the elves sitting on the lid made him feel short of breath himself.

"Hurry, Ashford. We need to do this now."

Ashford tore out the page he had been writing on, folded it and passed it to Alfie.

"If you can get this to Orin it might help us all. Give him this too." He pulled something from his pocket. Alfie took the small, worn velvet pouch. He felt sure he had seen one like it before.

"What is it?"

"Something I need Orin to fix for me. Now, are you ready?"

Alfie nodded.

"OK. Close your eyes," said Ashford softly. "Let everything but my voice slip away. Picture this room, but imagine Orin here. Imagine yourself being pulled back through into the past."

Alfie tried to do as Ashford asked, but visions of the elves stalking through his home kept slipping back into his mind. He drove them out and tried again.

"Focus, Alfie. You belong in Orin's time as much as this one, so for you to travel back I imagine you just need to relax and allow yourself to slip through time, as though you are going home."

It was easy for Ashford to say, but however much Alfie tried to relax, random thoughts and fears kept slipping into his head. It was starting to hurt. How could he just slip through time? It seemed impossible.

"Let's try something different," said Ashford at last. "Open your eyes. Remember the last two times you slipped?"

Alfie could hardly forget. The first time was when he was almost hit by a car. The second was when he lost consciousness as Murkle and Snitch chased him through a dark network of caves.

"What was the feeling you had in both of those moments?"

"I was scared. I knew I had to get out of there."

"More than that. What did you feel deep inside?"

Alfie thought hard, putting himself back in his own shoes. "I remember hearing my own heartbeat in my head. Time seemed to stretch out."

"Good. What else?"

"It was like those were my final seconds. I wanted to be some place else more than anything in the world. Then I got that feeling. You know, like when you're falling asleep and think you're falling, then you jerk awake? It was like that."

Ashford smiled. "Then that's the feeling you need to recreate. Close your eyes again."

Alfie did as he asked, hoping that Ashford knew what he was talking about.

"Now, notice your stomach. Remember the coldness that gripped it when you were running through the caves, when the car was speeding towards you?" Alfie let the sensation flow through him. "And your heart, feel it beating faster in your chest. Hear the blood pounding in your ears. Really feel it: the fear, the helplessness, the car screeching towards you."

Alfie was trying as hard as he could. He could feel his heart beating faster and an icy chill in his stomach. He was trying to imagine Murkle and

Snitch howling their way through the caves after him, but a little voice in his head kept reminding him that it wasn't real; he wasn't in danger. He tried to ignore it as he pictured himself back in the middle of the road, frozen in fear as he saw the horrified face of the driver in the car screeching towards him. He remembered his thoughts. It wasn't going to stop. It was going to hit him: he was going to die. At that moment something struck his chest so hard he went flying backwards.

He landed sprawling across the floor, and tried to work out what had happened as he untangled himself from the overturned footstool. Had Ashford kicked him over? He couldn't believe it. "Why did you do that?" he shouted as he scrambled to his feet. Alfie froze. It wasn't Ashford sitting in the armchair any more. It was someone else. A tall man in green robes, with kind eyes and a long, plaited beard.

Orin Hopcraft.

12

A Trip Through Time

Orin beamed as he put down his book and quill, wiped his inky fingers on his tunic and helped Alfie to his feet.

"I was hoping that it wouldn't be too long before you paid me a visit." He smiled as he righted the overturned footstool. "And that was quite an entrance."

Alfie went bright red. Ashford's plan had obviously worked, but he couldn't help being horrified that he had embarrassed himself in front of Orin Hopcraft.

"Sorry. I hope I'm not disturbing you?"

"No apology needed," said Orin, getting up and

reaching for a jar labelled Mugwort. "And you're not disturbing me at all. Take a seat and I'll make us some tea. I have a feeling you bring troubling news." Orin took several more jars of dried leaves and flowers from his shelves and measured them out into a kettle hanging above the fire. A sweet herbal aroma filled the room as he stirred the contents of the kettle and poured out two steaming cups of a greenish-yellow liquid. Alfie sniffed at his cup. He took a sip and felt every muscle in his body begin to relax.

"So, what brings you here?" asked Orin as he settled back into his armchair and fixed Alfie with his soft grey eyes. Alfie began to tell him everything that had happened over the last few days. The words tumbled over each other in their eagerness to get out as he told the story of the castle invasion, Ashford being dragged away, the sprite that had taken his place, the elves that were now roaming the castle's halls, Robin at risk of suffocating in the window seat, and the change magic Murkle and Snitch had left him with. Orin sat stroking one of the plaits in his beard as Alfie finally finished talking and waited for the druid to speak.

"Our word for oak tree is *daur* – door," he said at last. "Because they are doorways to other worlds, such as the elven realms. I have travelled through it myself during Samhain and Beltane when the borders between worlds are thin. It should not have been opened by one without the knowledge or foresight to close it properly – especially as that person has already angered the ruler of that realm. Ashford has been foolish beyond belief."

"You know Ashford?" asked Alfie.

Orin shook his head. "He cannot travel quite this far back, but I believe I will meet him at some point. I know of him, and his deeds, through Caspian."

"Can you help us?" asked Alfie. "You could leave a warning for Ashford, telling him not to go through."

"I'm afraid I can't interfere by trying to prevent this from happening," said Orin, his eyes grave. "Whatever warnings I leave for any of you in the future could just lead to events occurring in a different way. The Fates warned me of this. Some points in history cannot be changed." Alfie's heart dropped. He had been hoping that Orin would know exactly what to do and fix everything despite the six-hundred-year time difference.

"Ashford. How badly wounded is he?"

"Very. I think the wound is infected. It's making him really weak." Alfie handed over the letter and pouch that Ashford had given him. He sat quietly, studying the druid's face as he read the letter, wondering what it said.

At last Orin set the letter aside, placed the velvet pouch on his writing desk, and beckoned Alfie over to the table by the window. The druid cut sprigs from several of the herbs growing in pots on the window sill, and placed them into a stone mortar Alfie had last used when making a potion with Ashford, which revealed his evil headmistresses as a two-headed dragon.

"You know what to do?" he asked, handing Alfie the pestle. Alfie took it and began to mash the herbs to a paste. Orin unstopped several glass vials and added drops of strongly scented oils to the mixture. As Alfie mixed the oils into the paste, Orin took jar after jar from his crowded shelves, tipping small amounts of different herbs into the iron kettle over his fire. The study was soon full of a heady herbal scent that made Alfie feel as though everything might be OK.

When the herbs in the mortar were nothing but smooth paste, Orin scooped them out into a glass jar and chanted musical-sounding words over it. The mixture seemed to clarify, becoming the same slightly luminous green as the ointment that had healed Alfie's bruises at Muninn and Bone.

"I've seen this before," said Alfie. "We've used some of it on Ashford already. This is your recipe?"

Orin smiled. "I have shared it with a few, but only I can make it as powerful as this. Trust me, this will work." Before putting the top on the jar, Orin spooned a small amount into the brew in the kettle and stirred the potion briskly, nine times clockwise, then nine times widdershins. Using a cloth to carefully lift the kettle from the fire, he poured the steaming green liquid into a large stoneware jug.

"First, give him a draught of this tisane. It will send him to sleep for a couple of hours. Then clean the wound and apply this paste straight to it as a poultice."

"It'll make him better? Completely?" asked Alfie.

"I cannot say without seeing him for myself. But it should draw the poison from his system. When he wakes he will be stronger."

"Thank you, Orin," said Alfie, tucking the jar into his pocket and taking the jug, as well as a small sack into which the druid had packed a loaf of bread, some cheese and a flagon of water.

"Remember what I taught you last time you visited? How to let yourself be drawn home."

Alfie nodded and settled himself on the footstool, gripping the jug and sack tightly to ensure they travelled with him. Before he closed his eyes, the question that had been burning at the back of his mind sprang to his lips. "The change magic. I don't want it. Emily said you could help me get rid of it. Will you?"

"The creation magic I hid inside you when you were born could consume it to create something physical," said Orin. "That's how I built this castle. But it would not be wise for one with no magical training to try. That magic is best left sleeping. The more you use it the greedier it will become."

Alfie remembered the strange feeling he had as he tried to turn into his dad. "I could feel it watching me when I used the change magic. I think it wants to feed on it."

"I'm sure it does. All the more reason not to let it have its way, and to stop using the change magic. You are too young and inexperienced. Perhaps when your druidic training begins I can—"

"But Emily said I should practise..."

"Her advice was unwise."

"So I'm stuck with two magics that I don't want, and can't even use?" Alfie clenched his hands into fists as he spat out, "This isn't fair. I didn't even ask for any of this! People are getting hurt, because of me, because of the magic *you* gave me!"

Orin sighed. "I'm sorry. I burdened you even more than I realized when I hid the magic within you. But it was vital that it passed out of this time and into yours. Using it, especially untrained in magic, would bring great risk." He paused, pulling thoughtfully at his beard as if unsure whether to tell Alfie something. "Treat Ashford just as I have directed you," he said at last. "If you really want to get rid of the change magic, he may be the only person that can help you."

Alfie tried to read Orin's face, but he said no more on it.

"Tell Ashford I will do as he asks. He will find the item where he requested it to be left. Now go. Back to your own time."

Alfie had no trouble travelling back through the years this time. It was as though he just had to let his body be pulled through time to the space it should occupy in the future. He wondered if that was how he should think when travelling into the past, as though he was hopping between his own lifetimes.

There was a yell as Alfie materialized on the footstool, landing almost on Amy's knee. She jumped to her feet and tried to look as though she hadn't just shouted out in fright.

183

"Well done, Alfie!" said Ashford. "I'm sorry for kicking you over. I thought it would help you imagine you were in real peril." Alfie could hardly be cross with him – it had worked.

"How's Robin?" he asked, setting down the steaming jug and handing the bag of food to Amy.

"OK, for now," said Madeleine. "The elf is still sitting on the window seat, but we realized we could use the mirror to look inside it." She held out the mirror.

Alfie watched Robin carefully roll over into a more comfortable position inside the large chest. It must have been dark in there, but the mirror had some form of night vision allowing Alfie to see his cousin clearly. Better still, he could see a little shaft of light spilling through a small vent at the bottom of the chest. Alfie was sure it hadn't been there before.

"Nice one, Orin," he grinned.

"The others stopped searching a few minutes ago. They're eating now," said Madeleine, showing Alfie the Great Hall. All of the elves that weren't watching rooms and hallways were sitting around the table, eating what looked like the entire contents of Ashford's storeroom. The Queen was on her throne, stroking the beak of the silver sparrow on her shoulder as she ate flowers and berries from a small bowl. "Looks as though they're just going to wait us out."

"Alfie, did you give Orin the message?" asked Ashford, pulling the blanket tighter around his shoulders as he gave an involuntary shiver.

"I did. He said he'd do what you asked and will leave it where you wanted him to put it."

"So, are you going to tell us what it is, Ash?" Amy asked. "Seems like Alfie has earned that much."

"I can't," said Ashford. "But it will solve all of this if I take it to her." He pulled himself to his feet and began to stagger across the room. Alfie leapt up and held out his hands to block his path.

"Hey, slow down! You're not seriously thinking of going out there."

"I have to. I can make them leave."

Alfie stood firm as Ashford tried to push past him, but Amy and Madeleine helped guide him, protesting, back to the chair.

"See how weak you are?" said Alfie as Ashford tried and failed to stand up again. "If you can't even stand properly, how can you confront them?"

"But I can stop this," cried Ashford, holding tightly to Alfie's T-shirt.

"Then tell *me* where this thing is. If it will really make them leave, I can hand it over."

"No, you won't understand. I've got to do it."

Alfie realized that nothing was going to calm Ashford down, and changed his approach.

"OK. You can take it to them. But drink this first." He poured out a cup of the brew the druid had made. "Orin said it would strengthen you. If you're going to face them, you'll need it." He raised the cup to Ashford's lips.

"Then you'll let me go to them?" Ashford pleaded.

"I promise," said Alfie. "Now drink." No sooner had the butler drained the cup than he slumped back in the chair and began to snore gently.

Amy pulled up one of his eyelids. "He's out like a light. What did you do to him, Al?"

"He's OK," said Alfie, guilt stabbing at him for deceiving Ashford. "Orin said the tea would knock him out for a couple of hours while it drives out the poison." Ashford would be angry with him when he woke up, but there was no way Alfie was going to let him walk straight back into the elves' hands.

Opening the jar the druid had given him, Alfie peeled back Ashford's shirt. He undid the bandage on the butler's shoulder and stared at the wound underneath. Madeleine had done an excellent job of cleaning it. She had even applied little medical strips to hold the edges neatly together, but it still looked so raw. He began to apply the ointment in tiny dabs with his fingertip, flinching as he moved closer to the wound.

"Give it here," said Madeleine, swiping the jar from Alfie. She scooped out some of the ointment and smeared it carefully over the damaged skin. When she was satisfied, she began to bandage it back up.

"You're pretty amazing, you know that, Maddie?" said Amy.

"I know," said Madeleine in an offhand manner. But her cheeks flushed, and Alfie knew she was secretly delighted by the compliment. Galileo stretched out on his shelf and gave a sleepy meow, as though letting her know that he thought she was amazing too.

Alfie had almost forgotten about the walkie-talkie and nearly jumped out of his skin when he heard Robin's voice whispering from Orin's desk. He rushed over to grab it.

"Robin? What's going on?"

"What's wrong? Is he OK?" called Madeleine, hastily pinning the bandages.

"Are you looking at this room?" whispered Robin. "He's gone, hasn't he?"

Amy called up the workshop on the mirror. The elf that had been guarding his room was nowhere to be seen.

"Yes, he's gone," said Alfie.

"Right, I'm going to try to get up to you." Robin poked his head out of the chest. His hair was plastered to his forehead with sweat.

"Don't do anything stupid, Robin," said Alfie. "There are elves all over the place. There's even one in the library up here; you won't be able to get to us."

"Actually, he might," said Amy, showing Alfie the library in the mirror. It was empty. "They're all in the Great Hall."

Alfie glared at the elves in the mirror as they ate his food and drank wine from barrels they had dragged up from the cellars, laughing as the sprite that had impersonated Ashford capered around the room for the Queen's amusement.

"The difficult bit is going to be getting him past the doorway of the Great Hall."

Alfie watched as Amy checked the whole route from the workshop to the library. All of the elves had disappeared from their posts around the castle to join the party. As long as Robin could get past the hall without being seen, he would be able to reach to the library safely, unless...

"I don't see that evil-faced one, Merioch. Where is he?"

"He was out in the courtyard when you were visiting Orin," said Madeleine. "Sending back some of the elves that got sprayed with the iron filings. They looked pretty burnt. I haven't seen him since. I think he went through with them."

"Robin," Alfie said into the radio. "The coast is clear, but you need to go now. Stop when you get to the entrance hall. We'll let you know when it's safe to run past the Great Hall."

"OK," crackled Robin. "I'll turn the volume right down and hold it to my ear so they won't hear you. Now, am I clear to the entrance hall?"

"You are," said Alfie, images flashing in the mirror as Madeleine checked Robin's route.

"I won't talk to you again in case they hear. Follow me in the mirror and just say 'clear' when it's safe for me to pass the Great Hall." He put on his backpack, which looked very heavy. Alfie realized that Robin had filled it with the little iron-filing bombs and was holding a couple in his free hand. "Wish me luck," he whispered.

"Good luck!" Madeleine shouted as they watched Robin leave the room in a cautious crouching run.

"He's in the corridor. He's going up the steps. . ." Madeleine commentated needlessly as she clutched the mirror, knuckles white. Reaching the entrance hall, Robin looked up and pressed the radio to his ear.

"Wait," said Alfie. Madeleine called up the Great Hall, turning the mirror to look around the room. Most of the elves were at the table but several were milling around closer to the door. Alfie watched and waited, radio to his ear, ready to give the word. Amy got up and opened the inner door, positioning herself by the secret panel to open it for Robin.

Most of the elves were idly watching the sprite who was balancing anything he could find on to an elf who had fallen asleep slumped over an empty wine barrel. Finally a jug of water balanced on a teetering plate sent the whole pile cascading down, soaking the elf. Rudely awakened, he leapt to his feet, skidding and sliding on fruit and broken crockery. The Queen smiled lazily as the elf chased the sprite around the room, cheered on by the watching elves.

"Now, Robin. Go!" said Alfie, taking advantage of the chaos. Flicking back to the entrance hall, they watched Robin scurry past the doors unnoticed. Madeleine cheered as he started up the stairs. Ashford let out a little snort in his sleep at the noise.

"He's going to make it," she cried as Robin took the stairs two at a time. But Alfie had seen a movement against the wall at the top of the stairs. He looked closer. It was an elf, his skin glamoured to match the colour of the wall he was standing against.

"Robin, stop!" he called into the radio. Robin stopped dead still. Realizing he had been seen, the elf started towards him. Robin feinted right. When the elf moved in that direction Robin hurled the metal balls in his hands at the stone wall. They shattered, sending out a shower of iron filings and Madeleine punched the air in delight as Robin raced down the corridor to the library leaving the elf dancing around, shaking the iron from his burning skin.

Alfie scanned the shadows and his heart sank. Another camouflaged elf was waiting metres from the library.

"There's another, dead ahead," he shouted. Robin spun on his heel and ran in the opposite direction, towards Alfie's bedroom.

"Robin," said Alfie as his cousin hurtled towards his bedroom. "Hide in the secret bathroom in my bedroom, behind the panel to the right of the wardrobe. Push on the dark knot in the wood and the door will pop open, remember?"

Robin nodded as he ran. The elf slipped out of his glamour and began to charge after Robin. He was fast. Within seconds he had grabbed Robin's backpack. Not wanting to touch the chain-mail shirt, the elf tried to drag him to the stairs by his bag. Alfie held his breath as his cousin struggled to pull away, his walkie talkie dropping from his hand.

The stitching on the bag finally tore apart under the strain, sending a dozen of the metal balls crashing to the floor. The elf leapt out of the way, falling over the other who was running to join him, while still shaking the iron from his skin. Robin raced away as they both ended up in a heap.

"Ouch," said Amy. "I thought elves were supposed to be graceful?"

Madeleine changed the view to Alfie's room. Robin burst through the door and over to the panelled wall where he jabbed at the knot in the wood. The door to the secret room popped open.

"Watch out!" cried Alfie, who had seen

something move near his bed. The warning went unheard now that he had no way to communicate with his cousin. An arrow tore through Robin's sleeve, pinning his T-shirt to the woodwork. As he ripped it free, a shadow detached itself from the shadows of the bed curtains. Merioch. He raised his bow. Robin seemed to think twice about trying to slip through the secret door.

Alfie couldn't hear what the elf was saying, but it soon became obvious as Robin slowly removed his chain-mail shirt

The second the chain mail dropped to the floor, Merioch grabbed Robin by the wrist and dragged him from the room.

"No!" screamed Madeleine, sliding to her knees. Amy caught the mirror as it slipped from her hands.

Merioch glared his disapproval at the two elves picking themselves up from the floor. They followed him meekly as he dragged Robin down the stairs towards the Great Hall. Robin wasn't even bothering to struggle. After the way the elf had treated Ashford, Alfie thought his cousin was wise not to resist.

He watched the mirror helplessly as Amy closed the door to the study and rushed over to throw her arms around Madeleine, whose shoulders were shaking as silent tears splashed down on to her T-shirt. Alfie fought the urge to hit himself in the head. Why had he gone along with Robin's plan? He should have told him to stay where he was.

"Ashford said he had a way to end this," sobbed Madeleine. "We should have waited for him to wake up." Alfie felt worse than ever as he watched his cousin wiping her eyes and nose on her sleeve. She shrugged Amy's arm away and shook the butler by his one good shoulder.

"Wake up! Ashford, *please* wake up! We need you."

Alfie could see that it was no use; an earthquake wouldn't wake Ashford until the potion had worked its course. He eased Madeleine's hands off the butler and set her down on the footstool. Artan floated over and wrapped himself around her like a blanket.

Alfie picked up the mirror. "Great Hall." His voice shook as he wondered what they would see there. The elves were in a semicircle around Robin who had been pushed into a kneeling position before the Queen. She was holding something and seemed to be asking him a question. Robin answered and the Queen smiled and lifted the object to her mouth.

"I have one of yours." Alfie nearly dropped the walkie-talkie as a cold female voice crackled out of it. Amy and Madeleine stared at Alfie in horrified silence.

"Your friend refuses to tell us where you are, so I'm giving you one last chance to do the right thing. Give me what I want and I will return the boy, just as you remember him. If not, I will leave him to Merioch."

"You let him go right now!" screamed Madeleine, wrenching the walkie-talkie from Alfie's hand. "Do you hear me? Give him back, or *you'll* be the one who's sorry." Artan roared his agreement from her shoulder.

A cruel laugh rang out from the radio, echoed by the rest of the elves.

"Bring me the lens. Within the hour." Her voice cut through the air like a razor blade. "Or you'll hear every second of Merioch questioning your friend. One way or another, you *will* bring me what I want."

The radio went dead. Alfie quickly yanked it from Madeleine's hand to stop her throwing it across the room in rage.

"Let me out," roared Artan, floating to the door. "Let me go down there. I'll take Robin back from them! I'll snatch them up and drop them in the lake if they try to fight."

"Whoa there!" said Amy, leading Artan to the other side of the room to calm down while Alfie comforted Madeleine.

"So what are we going to do?" Madeleine asked. Her eyes flickered to the cord around Alfie's neck.

"Maddie, you know we can't just give them the talisman, right?" he said softly. "You saw what they did to Ashford. We can't trust them to let any of us go, and who knows what they're planning on using the crown for when they have the lens."

"OK, OK, I know," sighed Madeleine. "But we've got to do *something*."

"What was in the pouch that Ashford was going to take to them?" asked Amy. "Maybe we can find that? It sounded like something they would accept instead."

"I don't know," said Madeleine. "It was hidden in a little safe under a tile in his bedroom. He sent Robin down to fetch it while you two were out for your swim, but I don't know what it was. Do you think he asked Orin to put it back there?"

Alfie thought about it. "No. If Orin put it where

Robin found it that would probably create some kind of time loop. We're trapped in here, so this must be where he asked for it to be left." Alfie sighed as he looked around the room with its many cabinets and shelves crowded with books, jars, boxes and oddities. It could take days to search and he hadn't even found the keys to most of the little drawers and cupboards.

"But it'll take for ever to find if we don't even know what we're looking for!" sighed Amy.

Madeleine began searching anyway, going through all of the smaller items on the shelves one by one and asking if each could be the item Ashford was going to take to the Queen.

"No. I don't think so. Definitely not," Alfie answered patiently as she showed them a shark's tooth, a turquoise stone with a hole in it, a spiral fossil and a tiny jewelled bottle.

Alfie eventually left Amy to answer her and tried again to rouse Ashford. It was no use. He wasn't as pale, and he had stopped sweating and shivering, but he was out cold. Orin's potion was working. Alfie wished he could drink some himself and wake up to find that none of this had happened.

He picked up the mirror. Robin seemed fine

for the moment. He was sitting on a cushion by the Queen's feet, watching as she made the silver sparrow flit from one hand to the other and then peck at the fruit on her plate as if eating. Alfie scanned the rest of the castle. Elves had been stationed at lookout posts again but without their camouflage glamour. The Queen must be confident her ultimatum would work.

The elf that had been guarding the library was back in the chair by the fireplace, his head nodding drowsily. As Alfie watched him slowly falling asleep, an idea began to creep into his mind. It wasn't a particularly well-formed plan, and it would be incredibly difficult to pull off, but as the minutes ticked swiftly by it was the only thing he could think of. He had to rescue Robin and this seemed the only way. He called Madeleine and Amy over and explained his idea.

"You're sure?" asked Amy, watching the elf in the mirror as Alfie took off his shoes and quietly opened the inner door leading to the library. "Because there's no going back once we do this."

"I'm sure," said Alfie, against all the evidence his brain was sending him. He stepped into the little passageway between the library and the study. Madeleine followed, an arrow nocked to her bow.

The three of them stood just behind the panelled door to the library in their socks.

Artan floated inside the study, watching them gloomily. He had begged to be allowed to help, but Alfie was worried he might get overexcited. If the elf woke and had chance to warn the others they might as well just hand the talisman straight over.

Alfie put one hand on the panelled door ready to swing it open, the other tightly clutching a ball of thick, coarse twine he had found on Orin's shelves. He hoped it would be strong enough. Madeleine stood silently next to him, bow raised and half drawn. Amy put down the mirror and took up the cotton scarf she had used to cool Ashford's brow, holding one end in each hand.

"What if he calls our bluff over being ready to shoot him?" she whispered.

Alfie looked at the fierce set to Madeleine's jaw and the fire burning in her eyes.

"He'll believe we mean it," he whispered back. "Ready?" Madeleine and Amy nodded. Alfie opened the door. It swung outwards silently and they stepped through. Madeleine trained her arrow immediately on the elf, string held taut as the three of them advanced silently on the sleeping figure.

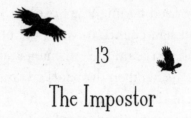

13

The Impostor

Alfie's heart was thumping so hard he was sure it would give them away, but the elf slumbered on as they crept closer. Madeleine stopped a few feet in front of the sleeping figure, arrow aimed at his forehead. Alfie took up a kneeling position by the chair. He held the string in one hand and gently grasped the bow lying across the elf's lap with the other. Amy crept around to reach over the back of the chair, her scarf held taut between two hands. She lowered it carefully until it was level with the elf's mouth, and then looked at Alfie. He nodded.

The elf sprang to life as Amy dragged the scarf between his lips, pulling his head tight against the back of the chair. His hands immediately grasped for his bow, but Alfie had pulled it from his lap and thrown it back across the room. He grabbed one of the elf's arms but the other hand was already closing around the hilt of a dagger at his hip.

Madeleine whistled.

The elf looked up to meet her eyes and froze at what he saw there. She shook her head and the elf slowly let go of the dagger and offered his hand to Alfie, who bound his wrists tightly together with the twine. With the elf subdued, Amy tied the ends of her scarf behind his head to complete the gag. He didn't take his eyes off Madeleine as they worked.

"Get up!" Alfie addressed their prisoner. The elf shot him a cold glance and remained seated.

"Maybe he doesn't understand English," said Amy.

"Stand!" Alfie mimed an upward motion with his hands. The elf scowled, but Madeleine made a slight movement as though about to release the arrow, and he sprang to his feet.

"This way," Alfie pulled on the twine and the elf grudgingly began to move, then froze as an ear-splitting yowl echoed around the room. A hissing, spitting ball of fur and claws launched itself through the air, knocking Madeleine's arm as it passed. Her fingers slipped on the bowstring and she let loose the arrow, sending it thudding into a bookcase.

"Leo!" yelled Alfie, as Amy grabbed the cat in mid leap, its claws raking the air in front of the elf's face. Before Madeleine could string another arrow, the elf made a dash for the library door. Alfie yelled as the twine whipped through his hands, burning a red line into his skin.

"Artan, fetch!" he called. The words were barely out of his mouth when the bear shot through out of the study and across the library, loose papers flying in his wake. The elf was reaching for the door handle as Artan barrelled into him, swiftly wrapping around him so that his head and shoulders were sticking out of one end, his feet from the other.

"Quick, get him inside," said Alfie. "They might have heard us." Artan carried his carefully wrapped package through the air and into the study after Madeleine and Amy. Alfie grabbed the elf's bow and chased Galileo back through the secret entrance, closing the door carefully behind them. Grabbing the mirror, he checked the hallways and heaved a sigh of relief to see that none of the elves seemed aware there had been any commotion in the library.

"Well done, Artan," he said, patting the grinning bear on the head as Amy and Madeleine high fived over the squirming elf. "Hold him there while I get his clothes." Alfie pulled off the struggling elf's boots and trousers then tied his ankles with the twine. Galileo sat nearby, cleaning behind his ears as Alfie worked. "And you!" he pointed one finger at the cat. "When we get out of this there'll be no tuna for a whole year!" The cat stretched nonchalantly and slunk away to curl up by the fire.

"I'm done here," said Alfie when he was satisfied with his knots. "Put him in the chair by the writing desk." Artan deposited the bound elf and Alfie passed the twine to Madeleine to tie him to the chair, which he noticed she went about none too gently. Alfie unbuckled their captive's leather breastplate. He had to untie the elf's hands to get the tunic he wore under his leather armour, but Amy and Madeleine held his wrists tightly and Artan floated in front of him, growling so menacingly that the elf didn't move a muscle to resist. Soon he was tightly bound to the chair in his long undergarments. Alfie changed into his clothes in the garderobe. He felt uncomfortable removing the chain-mail shirt, and losing the protection it offered against the elves, but if his plan was to work he couldn't be discovered wearing it.

"Are you sure you can do this, Al?" said Amy as Alfie shuffled into the room, feeling slightly ridiculous in clothes and boots that were far too big for him.

"Yes," said Alfie firmly. If he was going to protect his home and his family, he had to use the change magic. "How long have we got?"

"Nineteen minutes," said Madeleine. "Providing she's going to stick to one hour."

Alfie positioned a chair just far enough away from the elf that he could take in his whole form at once and sat down. The elf watched him as if he wished he could burn him alive with his glare. He took some calming breaths and stared at the elf, taking in every aspect of his appearance. Orin wouldn't be happy about what he was doing, but he didn't see any other way. It wasn't as if the druid had offered any other solution.

It was difficult to concentrate with the elf's malevolent eyes burning holes into him, but he reached deep inside and prodded the change magic awake, letting it rush through him until the skin all over his body began to tingle, as though awaiting instructions.

He remembered Emily's training. Instead of trying to force himself to change, he imagined he was a mirror reflecting back the figure sitting in front of him. Wearing the elf's clothes made the job easier. All he had to get right were the head, hands, height and body shape.

He knew it was starting to work when his ears began to tingle. He felt them change shape, becoming slightly larger and pointed, amplifying Amy and Madeleine's gasps and amazed whispers. Alfie blocked them out as he focused. The clothes he was wearing started to feel more fitted as he grew taller and broader; his feet seemed less lost in the soft leather boots. His scalp tickled as his hair grew longer, flowing down over his shoulders in pale blonde locks. He scrutinized the elf's face, feeling his features becoming more angular. Finally, he concentrated hard on turning his irises pale gold. The elf's face twisted into an even darker scowl, and Madeleine and Amy burst into applause. Alfie knew his disguise was complete.

"How do I look?" he asked, his voice strangely distorted in his new larger body.

"Perfect," said Amy, slapping him on the back.

"Apart from the expression. Try imagining that we're all something nasty you just stepped in." Alfie glared down his long nose at her. "There! You've got it!"

"Alfie, you forgot something," said Madeleine from behind him.

"What?" said Alfie, turning to see her fist flying towards his new face. It connected with his jaw with a *smack* that made his teeth clack together painfully. "OW! What did you do that for?"

"Sorry," said Madeleine, squaring up for another punch. "I thought it would be easier if I didn't warn you. You can't speak Elvish, so there should be a reason why you can't speak. Hold still, I hardly got you there. You need a much more believable bruise than that."

Alfie caught Madeleine's fist. "Maddie, you idiot!" he said, rubbing his jaw. "You just watched me transform into an elf. Didn't you think I could manage a little bruise the same way?"

Madeleine's face dropped. "Oh! I'm so sorry, Alfie."

"It was actually a great idea," smiled Amy. "But maybe share the plan with us first next time."

Alfie shook his head crossly, then looked into a mirror on the wall and let his cheek and jaw swell and turn a spectacular shade of purple.

"Nice!" said Amy when he had finished. "No one could expect you to speak with a face like that. So then, which of us is coming as your prisoner?"

"Me!" said Madeleine firmly.

"What do you mean?" asked Alfie, stringing the elf's bow and quiver over his shoulder.

"Wait ... you weren't planning on going down there on your own and trying to grab Robin in a room full of elves, were you?" said Amy.

Alfie shrugged. His plan hadn't really progressed much further than that. "I thought Artan could swoop down to the window behind where the Queen is sitting. I'll hang about there and look for a chance to grab Robin and we'll jump out of the window on to Artan. He can take us up to the eastern tower. They haven't found the way up there so we'd be safe until Ashford wakes up and does whatever he was planning to do to stop them."

Artan clapped his paws. "Excellent plan, lad. We'll be up and away before they know what happened."

"I don't think so," said Madeleine, showing Alfie the Great Hall in the mirror. "Who do you see standing next to the Queen?"

Alfie's heart dropped. "Merioch."

"Exactly," said Amy. "It looks like no one gets

close to her except her right-hand man. You're not going to be able to hang around near Robin looking shifty. But if you had a prisoner with a penknife hidden in their sock..." she grinned, "they'd be put with Robin and could cut their ropes and untie him too."

"Yeah, then you could make a distraction and I'll get Robin to Artan," said Madeleine.

"What makes you think it should be you?" said Amy.

"He's my brother," said Madeleine.

"But I'm faster at running."

"No you're not!"

Alfie watched them bicker, amazed that they were fighting over taking part in a plan which was making his blood run cold. He had to admit that their idea was better than his, providing he could slip away unnoticed after the rescue.

"We don't have time for this," he said at last. "Amy, you're coming with me."

"No!" Madeleine shouted in anger as Amy grinned.

"Not because she's any better than you," he said quickly, as Madeleine looked as if she was squaring up to hit him again. "Maddie, you need to keep an eye on our prisoner here, and if Ashford gets worse you can help him better than any of us. When he wakes up you need to tell him what's going on. If this goes wrong, he's our last hope."

Madeleine grudgingly accepted the importance of her role and tied Amy's hands loosely behind her back.

Alfie slipped a small knife into Amy's sock, then removed his talisman and handed it to Madeleine. "Look after this," he said, and then gave her his walkie-talkie. "And you're going to need this."

Looking as cold and confident as the elf was harder than Alfie thought as he strode out of the library and down the corridor in a body that felt all wrong, pushing Amy along in front of him. Luckily the path to the stairs and down to the first floor was clear. When he reached the landing he looked swiftly around, took Amy's walkie-talkie from her belt, opened the visor of a suit of armour and dropped it inside. He knew Madeleine would be watching and hoped he could rely on her to play her part at the right time.

"Ready, Amy?" he whispered. He began to drag her down the rest of the stairs as she struggled and kicked out at him.

"Get *off* me! Let me *go!*" she hollered.

Elves ran out to see the cause of the commotion

and laughed to see one of their number with a grossly swollen face struggling with a young girl. Remembering his character, Alfie scowled viciously at them and dragged Amy into the Great Hall.

Merioch stood up and the Queen clapped her hands with joy as Alfie brought Amy before her. He handed over a knife he had grabbed from Orin's study to indicate he had disarmed her.

"Amy!" Robin shouted, struggling to get to his feet, his face a mask of horror to see Amy captured too. Merioch pushed him back down and prowled around Alfie and his prisoner. Alfie couldn't tell if he was suspicious or just trying to intimidate. He barked something in Elvish. Alfie shook his head and pointed to his swollen jaw, but Merioch wasn't satisfied. He spoke again and Alfie let out an indistinct mumble. This only seemed to make him angrier.

"He can't answer you," shouted Amy, looking up at the elf defiantly. "You wouldn't be able to talk either after an iron glove to the face."

The corner of Merioch's mouth turned up into a humourless smile as he regarded Alfie.

"I've always said Loth was too slow to catch his own breath," he sneered, waving Alfie away. Alfie took a seat at the closest end of the table trying to hear what was being said over the derisive laughter of the elves around him. Either Loth wasn't popular, or the other elves wanted to ingratiate themselves with Merioch. Alfie suspected it was both. He glared at them, glad that they seemed to have accepted his disguise completely.

"Time is up," said the Queen. "Have you brought the lens in exchange for your friend?"

"No," said Amy as Merioch made a move to search her. "*He* already checked me for it." She nodded towards Alfie who shook his head to signify he hadn't found it. "It'll be here soon though," she added quickly as the Queen's face began to cloud over. "Alfie needs to get it from where it's hidden. He sent me to tell you he'd bring it soon." She let her lower lip quiver. "Please don't hurt us."

Alfie thought Amy was doing a great job of sounding afraid, but with Merioch standing over her he imagined that most of her fear was real. The storm passed from the Queen's face and she smiled sweetly. "I hope so, little one. I would hate to watch Merioch hurt either of you. Now sit by me. We'll soon see if your friend is really on his way."

Merioch dragged Amy over to sit next to Robin as the Queen picked up Robin's walkie-talkie again. Alfie had to stop himself jumping up as he realized her voice would echo out through the radio he had hidden in the armour and ruin his plan. How could he stop her using it without raising suspicion? He gripped the edge of the table, his knuckles turning white as the Queen spoke into the radio. He let out his breath in a gasp as the Queen shook it and then tossed it aside to smash on the flagstones. The battery was dead; his plan could still work. Robin had noticed Alfie's reaction and said something in Amy's ear. She whispered back and Robin's eyes widened in amazement. He quickly looked away from Alfie so as not to draw suspicion.

"No whispering," tutted the Queen, tapping Amy lightly on the nose. "Your communication device no longer works, but the clock is ticking." She smiled and made a ticking motion with her finger then went back to playing with the little silver sparrow. Alfie was glad to see Merioch stride out of the room. He imagined it was to find whoever was bringing the talisman so that he could take it and claim the credit himself.

Amy leant back slightly. Alfie hoped she'd be able to get the knife out of her sock. She shuffled closer to Robin. Alfie guessed it would take her a couple of minutes to cut through Robin's ropes. He hoped Madeleine was watching the mirror and ready to act. The walkie-talkie had been a close call.

A dark shadow flitted past the window. Alfie stiffened, but none of the other elves had seen Artan swoop down to float just below the window ledge. Alfie looked to Amy and she gave him a little nod to indicate she had cut their bonds and they were ready to go. He stood up and stretched as though his arms and back were stiff, hoping that Madeleine would spot the signal. She did.

Almost immediately a strange moaning floated down from the first floor. The elves were laughing and shouting too loudly over the table to notice, so Alfie let out an unintelligible shout and cupped his hand to his ear. The table went quiet as the eerie moans echoed through the castle like an angry ghost, growing louder and louder. Arming themselves with their bows, the elves hurried to the entrance hall. Merioch was standing on the bottom step, staring up at the suit of armour inside which Alfie had hidden the walkie-talkie.

Alfie remained just inside the Great Hall to watch Amy and Robin. Madeleine was certainly throwing her all into the screeches and yells echoing out from the armour. None of the elves seemed to want to go anywhere near it. He assumed that the story of the animated suits of armour at Muninn and Bone's offices had spread. The Queen finally decided that the disturbance was worthy of her attention and left her throne to view the situation for herself.

Amy immediately leapt up and ran for the window, Robin limping slowly and painfully behind as though his legs had gone to sleep after kneeling for so long.

Alfie held his breath as he tried to keep one eye on the elves and the other on Amy and Robin. Amy was struggling with the stiff iron latch on one of the huge leaded windows. The more Alfie's heart pounded in his chest, the harder it was to stay in disguise. His disguised skin itched as he tried to calm his nerves.

Merioch shouted and the elves took aim at the wailing armour. Giving up on the first window, Amy moved to another and finally managed to unlatch it. Alfie could hear Merioch counting down in Elvish. Just as Amy and Robin managed to open the window the elves let loose their arrows, peppering the armour's breastplate like a pincushion

The armour slowly toppled forwards and came crashing down the stairs in pieces. "Come on!"

Alfie whispered under his breath as Amy boosted Robin up to the window ledge. Elves jumped out of the path of the pieces of iron bouncing towards them, and Alfie leapt about with them, purposefully jostling the ones that looked close to turning around and seeing Amy and Robin's escape.

A shout from Merioch silenced the chaos. He had found the walkie-talkie that had fallen from the armour and held it out to the Queen. Realization that they had been tricked dawned on their faces. Spinning around, the Queen saw Robin scrambling out of the window. She shouted a curse so strong that a passing fly dropped out of the air stone dead.

Alfie pretended to trip on a chest plate and fell back into the elves rushing towards the hall. They began to topple over each other as Amy pushed Robin out on to Artan's back and pulled herself up on to the ledge. Merioch walked over the backs of the elves that had fallen to the floor and took an arrow from his quiver.

Alfie leapt up and charged into him as he raised his bow. The effect was like hitting a stone statue, but he managed to redirect the elf's aim and the arrow smashed through one of the tiny windowpanes to the left of Amy. She cast a desperate glance back at Alfie then hurled herself out of the window and on to Artan. The bear whisked Amy and Robin away as more elves recovered enough to send arrows crashing uselessly after them.

Merioch hurled elves out of his path and grabbed Alfie by his tunic, shouting something in his own language. Alfie mumbled and pointed to his swollen mouth, but this time Merioch wanted an answer.

The prickling that had started in Alfie's skin intensified as the elf disguise began to slip. He struggled but Merioch was impossibly strong. Alfie felt as though his brain was rattling against his skull as the elf shook him violently. As Merioch lifted him into the air, Alfie finally gave up the effort of keeping his disguise.

Expecting to shrink back to his usual size, Alfie was shocked to find himself growing. Merioch's cold mask slipped as something in Alfie's face seemed to frighten him. Alfie crashed painfully to the floor as the elf hurled him away. The Queen was shouting and something was growling. Getting to his feet, Alfie realized that the growl was coming from his own throat. He was shooting up in size, bursting out of Loth's clothes as his body turned green and scaly. Merioch shouted again and the elves let their arrows fly as Alfie watched his hands twist into vicious-looking claws. The change magic had taken control, he realized. It was protecting itself, just as Orin's magic had. He was becoming a dragon.

Alfie felt a cold satisfaction as the arrows clattered harmlessly off his scales. He tried to shout, but a terrible roar burst from his jaws and he felt something burning in his belly... *Flames?* The elves were in disarray. Some of them had run for the portal, others cowered in the corners of the hall. The bravest encircled him, firing arrow after arrow. Alfie span around clumsily, his tail sweeping their legs from under them. Arrows bounced off him as he charged, driving some of them out towards the destroyed doorway. Maybe he could scare them from his castle.

The burning in his stomach intensified. He knew he'd feel better if he released the flames. He felt angry. *They invaded my home, threatened my family, tortured Ashford.* He had never felt such rage. But as the fire bubbled up into his throat, the shreds of himself that remained fought back against the dragon-like fury. He couldn't kill. He couldn't burn the castle with everyone inside. Alfie roared and fought back against the anger, bellowing in pain. His huge body doubled over as he struggled to contain the fire inside him.

The elves stopped firing and ran from his great stomping feet and thrashing tail as he tried to control himself. He clutched his great scaly head with his claws, summoning every ounce of mental strength, and tried to shut down the change magic.

"NOOOOO!" he yelled, the sound coming out as a distorted growl as he staggered forwards. The ground rushed up to meet him as he rapidly shrank in size, his skin regaining its colour as he collapsed to the floor and sank into unconsciousness.

14

The Tower and the Crown

When Alfie awoke he was surrounded by armed elves, their arrows trained on his head. They all stood a few metres back, presumably in case he metamorphosed into a dragon again. Very slowly, he sat up and tied the torn tunic he had been wearing back around himself. The Queen and Merioch stood shoulder-to-shoulder, drawing amusement from his embarrassment.

"You are him," said the Queen. "Alfie – the keeper of the lens. *My* lens."

"Yes," said Alfie. There was no point in trying to deny it. Thirty elves drew back their bows as he got to his feet. The Queen held up a finger and they relaxed their strings slightly.

"I can see you don't have it with you," she said to a chorus of laughter from the elves. "So, where is it?"

"Somewhere safe," said Alfie. Goose pimples prickled across his bare skin as he clutched the tunic around himself.

"Enough time-wasting," said Merioch angrily. "You will tell us where it is."

"No," said Alfie, amazed that he managed to keep his voice level as he tried to stand tall and defiant in nothing but a torn piece of cloth. "I'm not taking you any—" the words died in his throat as an arrow whizzed past his cheek, grazing his skin just enough for a drop of blood to run down his face and drip on to his bare toes. He felt the ancient magic Orin had hidden within him flicker to life at the threat. *Not you too*, he thought to himself. It had been hard enough controlling the change magic.

"If your next answer is not the location of the lens," Merioch hissed down the length of an arrow notched to his bow, "this arrow will pierce your heart."

"Then we will tear this castle apart stone by stone until we find it. And your friends," purred the Queen in a voice so pleasant she might have been offering him a slice of cake. Alfie swallowed hard. Her words struck even more fear into his heart than Merioch's had. What could he do? He couldn't tell them where the talisman was without revealing Madeleine and Ashford, who wouldn't even be awake to defend himself. And what else would the elves find in Orin's study that they could put to terrible use?

The Queen stepped back. Every elf pulled back their bow. "You have five seconds," she smiled. "One."

Alfie's heart hit his ribs. What could he do?

"Two."

The magic flexed its might by sending an electric jolt through Alfie's nerve endings as it prepared to defend its host.

"Three."

He fought against the raw power rising inside him. He couldn't use it, not without the talisman. It would tear him apart in trying to save him.

"Four."

Alfie closed his eyes, his whole body vibrating with uncontrolled magical energy. Should he stop fighting to keep it under control? He was going to die anyway.

"Fi—"

"STOP!" Running footsteps echoed through the

hall. Alfie kept his eyes clenched shut, fighting to control the energy that had been ready to explode out from his body. The Queen stopped her count and the elves began to hoot with excitement. The magic grudgingly let Alfie rein it back as the immediate danger lifted. He risked opening his eyes. The elves were facing a small figure who was holding her arm out towards the Queen.

"Maddie!" he cried. Amy and Robin had got away safely, yet here she was, risking her life for him. With the bows no longer pointing at him, Alfie took a step towards his cousin and froze in alarm as he saw what was dangling from her fist. The talisman. Its purple lens glimmered as it swung from side to side. The Queen watched it greedily, like a snake about to strike.

"Let Alfie go and I'll give you the lens," said Madeleine.

"You are hardly in a position to bargain."

"Hush, Merioch." The Queen smiled. "Let the boy go to her." Merioch's eyes narrowed as Alfie hurried over to his cousin, unable to believe that she had brought them the talisman despite being told it must never fall into their hands.

"I saw you needed these." She passed Alfie some jeans and a sweatshirt. Alfie dressed under cover of the torn tunic, his gratitude for the clothes doing nothing to diminish his fury at her for bringing the talisman right to them.

"Now. The lens." The Queen whistled and pointed her finger. The silver sparrow fluttered from her shoulder to Madeleine's hand and pecked at the talisman's string.

"Don't give it to her!" pleaded Alfie.

"It's OK," whispered Madeleine, letting the bird take the string in its beak. Alfie couldn't believe what she had done as the bird fluttered back to the Queen whose laughter filled the hall as she received her prize.

"You've got what you came for," said Alfie, "so now you'll leave and go home?"

The Queen laughed again. Even Merioch cracked a smile.

"Of course we'll leave," she trilled.

"And you'll let us go?" said Alfie. "All of us?"

"You and your friends will all remain in Hexbridge."

Something about the Queen's voice didn't inspire Alfie with confidence. He waited for a "but".

"But . . . I like this castle. I've decided it will be my new home."

"You said you were leaving," shouted Madeleine,

her hands clenched tightly by her sides.

"We are. But the castle is coming with us. This land of yours, Hexbridge, will be the first addition to our own lands. Its people will accept me as their Queen. Life for them will be very much the same, except they will worship me and do everything I ask."

"Maddie already gave you *my* talisman. Isn't that enough? Why can't you just leave us alone?"

"*Your* talisman?" said the Queen, shadows crossing her face and emphasizing its sharp features. She held up the talisman. "This unworthy receptacle for a lens destined to take its place in *my* crown?"

Winds that Alfie couldn't feel swept her hair out around her face like angry snakes. As she towered in front of him Alfie could see the empty hole in the centre of the jewelled circlet upon her head, its other stones glowing gently as though great power lay within.

"Stolen by a pathetic thief who took *two* of my most prized possessions and then dared to return to our lands once more, to steal again no doubt!"

She waved her hand and Merioch seized Madeleine's shoulders, while the sprite grabbed Alfie's arms tightly.

"We have one of yours," Alfie shouted suddenly.

"Loth. The one I was disguised as. Let us go and my friends will release him."

"They can throw him into the lake with rocks tied to his feet," sneered the Queen. "I have no time for incompetence." Alfie crumpled as his last hope faded away. "Now, you will show us to one of the towers. The one to the east, which looks down over the village, will do nicely."

"No," said Alfie. The Queen nodded at Merioch, who drew a dagger from his belt and pressed it to Madeleine's neck so swiftly Alfie barely had time to shout, "STOP! I'll take you. Let her stay here and I'll take you."

"We *all* go," said the Queen, sweeping towards the door. "Bring them."

Alfie was shoved roughly forwards as the elves marched up the stairs. He bit his lip so hard it began to bleed as he led them towards the tower. The hallways and secret passages of the castle ran through his head as he tried to plot out a route to take them on that would give him a chance of escaping along the way. He considered dashing away and barricading himself into one of the rooms they passed, but the arrows pricking his back stopped him. Even if he could get away he would be leaving Madeleine behind. For a terrible, guilty second he wondered if that wasn't such a bad idea. He glared at her as they climbed the stairs to the second floor.

"Why? Why did you bring the talisman? I left it there so that it would be safe from them."

"It's not what you think," she whispered out of the corner of her mouth as Merioch pushed her forwards. "Ashford *wanted* them to have it."

"Silence," snapped Merioch as they climbed the final flight of stairs. Alfie glared at Madeleine. How could she even know what Ashford wanted? Unless he'd woken up and told her to take the talisman in order to save himself. Maybe he was escaping the castle right now. He couldn't believe Madeleine had been so stupid. She glanced at him as though she wanted desperately to say something, then shook her head and looked away.

"I see no door," said the Queen, as they reached the stone carving at the end of the corridor.

Merioch bent forwards and hissed in Alfie's face. "Open it."

Alfie crossed his arms. He wouldn't tell them how to open the entrance. Merioch bent down until he was nose to nose with Alfie, grabbed him by the neck and growled "OPEN IT!"

"Put him down!" cried Madeleine as Alfie

coughed and struggled against the elf. Merioch whirled around, grasped Madeleine's hair, and yanked her head back so sharply that she couldn't help crying out in pain.

"You don't have to open it, Alfie," she gasped. Merioch lifted her by the hair until her legs were kicking out in mid air.

Alfie knew he had no choice. How could Madeleine have been so reckless? She couldn't possibly have thought that giving the talisman to the Queen was the right thing to do. He took a deep breath and pressed the four bricks in order. The torches on the wall sprang to life as the wall parted to reveal the entrance to the tower. Merioch dropped Madeleine and pushed Alfie through the entrance as the other elves poured through around them. Alfie tried to contain his rage as they shot up the spiral staircase, rampaging through the room of treasures Orin had collected from around the world.

"Leave these trinkets!" snarled the Queen. "There will be time for this when the castle is within our own realm." Merioch pushed the stragglers out of the room and they filed up the stairs to the top of the tower. The sprite held on to Alfie and Madeleine's arms to stop them running back down. As they climbed through the trapdoor at the top Alfie saw that the misty dome still hung over the castle, keeping it in perpetual twilight.

"Time to view our new domain," the Queen smiled to Merioch. She waved her arms in a complicated motion and the mist began to swirl as though she were running her fingers through it. Slowly, it flowed down into the courtyard and back through the oak portal.

As the dome disappeared, Alfie could make out the outline of the hills and forest against the night sky. Only a few street lights lit the sleeping village below. Straining his eyes, Alfie wondered if he could see a light from Merryweather farm, far in the distance. Was his dad there, with Granny and the twins' parents? Soon they would all be together again, as slaves in another realm.

The Queen whistled and dozens of fireflies swarmed up to the tower, floating gently above it like a constellation of green and yellow stars. The silver sparrow on her shoulder snapped its little beak at any that flew too close. Under their soft light, the Queen removed her crown and handed it to Merioch to hold. She removed the lens from the talisman and inserted it into the hole in the crown. All of the jewels seemed to shimmer more brightly in its presence.

"With this lens, the power of all the other

gems is focused." She spoke directly to Alfie, her beautiful face ghostly green in the light of the fireflies. "Through it I will expand my realm until all living things call me their Queen. She tucked the empty talisman into Alfie's pocket and patted him on the head.

Alfie's hand twitched towards the crown, but the sprite held his arms so tightly that all thoughts of grabbing it and hurling it down into the lake melted away. The Queen shook her head and tapped him on the nose with her finger, then reached to take it back from Merioch. Her face changed as he didn't let go.

"What game is this?" she asked, trying to wrench it from his hands. Merioch pushed her back with one hand, his face impassive as he held the crown high above her head. "Seize him," she screamed, jumping up to try and grab it.

Alfie was reminded of the bullies at his last school as he watched Merioch taunting the Queen with her own crown. She stopped trying to reach it as she realized that none of the elves were obeying her command. "Was I not clear?" She held herself tall as she tried to recover her composure. "I said *seize him*." She pushed one of the elves in front of her.

Merioch clicked his fingers. Two of the elves behind him stepped forwards and grasped the Queen's arms.

"Traitors!" she screamed in fury. "Traitors. All of you. May your blood boil and your skin shrivel—" She stopped mid-sentence as Merioch placed his finger on her lips and gently touched his knife to her face. Her eyes shot fire at him as he pushed her over to Alfie and Madeleine, just another prisoner.

Alfie could feel cold fury radiating from the Queen as she stood next to him watching Merioch raise the crown and place it on his own head. He wondered if Ashford was awake, if he was watching through Orin's mirror. He thought about Robin and Amy in Artan's tower. What would happen to them when Hexbridge was pulled into the elven realms? They couldn't stay hidden for ever. What would happen to his dad, to Granny, Aunt Grace and Uncle Herb? Would he ever get to go to school and see all of his friends again, or would they all become Merioch's slaves? Or worse, his army.

The grip on Alfie's shoulder lessened as the sprite stared up at the crown on Merioch's head, its gems glowing brightly. Madeleine nudged Alfie's arm with her own.

"I'm sorry," she whispered. "They were going

to shoot you, I had to do something. I didn't think they'd bring us with them when they tried to use it."

Alfie watched Merioch raise his fingers to his temples in concentration. The crown began to emit a low thrumming noise as it lit the whole top of the tower with a purple glow.

"Doesn't matter really, does it?" said Alfie. "We're going with them whether we're up here or down there."

Madeleine smiled grimly and shook her head. "Not exactly."

The thrumming changed to a high-pitched piercing whine. Merioch staggered backwards. Something was wrong. The lens in the centre of the crown was swirling like a tiny galaxy, or something more sinister – a black hole. Alfie realized it was growing fast. A wind started blowing around them and the fireflies whirled away, disappearing into the expanding hole in the crown. The elf fell to his knees and tried to prise the crown from his head. It was stuck fast.

The sprite let go of Alfie and Madeleine as the swirling wind blew stronger, sucking bows, arrows and everything that wasn't securely attached into the gaping hole. Alfie tried to get to the trapdoor but jumped back as he was almost trampled by the panicking elves fighting each other to pull it open. A piercing screech rang out, and Alfie turned to see the sprite being sucked into the hole, his body appearing to stretch and distort as he disappeared screaming into blackness.

Staggering to the edge of the tower, Alfie hung on to one of the stones of the battlements. Madeleine was hugging the one next to him. He could feel his feet starting to lift into the air as the crown pulled him towards it.

"Hang on!" he shouted to Madeleine over the screams of elves tumbling into the hole behind them.

Alfie wondered if he dared jump off the tower. Surely falling to his death would be better than being sucked through into that terrible nothingness.

A faint hope flickered inside him. Would Artan be able to hear him over the roaring wind? Holding tight to the stone with one arm, he reached into his pocket and found the silver whistle. He clenched it between his lips and blew as hard as he could. Grabbing Madeleine's arm, he made a gesture with his hand to indicate going over the edge.

Fighting the wind, Alfie began to pull himself

on to the tower wall. Madeleine seemed to consider her limited options and then did the same. Dragging himself forwards until he was sitting on the edge of the battlements, Alfie leaned forwards over the dizzying drop to the courtyard below; only the hungry gravity of the crown kept him from plummeting to earth. He blew again and again on the whistle, the screams of the elves growing fewer as one by one they were swallowed by the void. Now the very stones of the castle were beginning to vibrate, mortar crumbling as they came apart.

In the darkness there was no way to tell whether or not Artan was coming. Alfie grabbed for Madeleine's hand. She met his eyes and shrugged as though to say *might as well*. Together they leapt, launching themselves away from the collapsing tower. Castle stones swirled away into the void behind them as they fell in slow motion away from the pull of the crown.

An animal roar grew rapidly closer as their fall increased in speed, the earth's gravity replacing that of the crown.

"Aaaartaaaan!" screamed Alfie as he saw the bear speeding towards them as the courtyard loomed below. Seconds before they smashed into the cobbles Artan swept under them and they bounced on to his back. The bear carried them gently down into the garden where they lay panting on the grass.

Looking straight up, Alfie saw the top floors of the tower implode, sucked into the centre of the crown. Only Merioch was left, hovering high up in mid-air before he stretched, distorted, and was finally swallowed by the crown himself. As he vanished the crown seemed to fold in on itself, disappearing with a little pop, leaving the night still and silent once more.

15

Ashford's Question

An angry shout brought Alfie back to reality. "Release me!" a woman was screaming. He sat up to see Artan wrapped tightly around the Queen, who was trying to hop towards the portal in the oak tree.

"This one hitched a ride on the way down," Artan grinned. "Want me to throw her in the lake?"

"What, and pollute it?" shouted Robin, who had run out of the castle doors followed by Amy and Ashford. "Why don't you find a nice hot volcano instead?"

"Happy to oblige," said Artan, rising into the air.

"No you don't!" said Alfie, grabbing one of the

bear's paws and pulling him back to earth. "Just set her down over there until we can figure out what to do."

"I can't believe you got out of that, mate," said Amy, looking up at the ruins of the eastern tower. "I thought you'd be... Well you could have been..." She gave up trying to form a sentence and flopped down on to the grass between Alfie and Madeleine, wrapping her arms around their shoulders. Even Robin and Ashford hurried over to join in the group hug. Artan looked very disappointed to be left out so they all ruffled his fur and scratched him under the chin, ignoring the bedraggled Queen in his grasp.

"I don't understand what happened," said Alfie, finally escaping the scrum and pulling his empty talisman from his pocket. "Why didn't the lens work?"

"Because it wasn't your talisman he gave them," said Madeleine. Alfie stared at her in confusion.

"She's right," said Ashford, dropping something into Alfie's hand. Another talisman. "This one is yours." Alfie turned it over, comparing it to the other talisman. Apart from the missing lens they were exactly the same, even down to a tiny scratch on the back.

"You asked Orin to make a fake?" he asked Ashford as it dawned on him at last.

"I figured it out!" interrupted Madeleine, practically bouncing on her knees. "Ashford wouldn't wake up, so I had a brilliant idea! I got a pencil and rubbed it over the page under the one he had written on in the notebook. It revealed what he'd written. He asked Orin to replace the crystal lens in the talisman with coloured glass, and to hide it under the inkwell pot set into the desk in the study. And I found it. I knew it was safe to give it to them, because the lens wasn't real. Orin left the original lens in here with it!" Madeleine pulled the little velvet pouch that Alfie had taken to Orin from her pocket and shook it.

"Go, Madds!" said Amy, giving her a high five.

Alfie scratched his head as he stared at the two talismans in his hand. "I still don't understand. Why was there another talisman, and why did the lens need replacing? Wasn't the whole thing a fake in the first place?"

"No. It's just as real as yours." Everyone looked at Ashford as he took the empty talisman from Alfie and the lens from the pouch Madeleine was holding and fixed the two back together. "This one is mine." He fastened the repaired talisman around his neck.

Alfie was confused. "How can it be? Emily told me mine is one of a kind."

"And she was speaking the truth," said Ashford.

Alfie continued to stare at him blankly. Was the butler still delirious?

"So you're telling us you're both wearing the same talisman?" said Robin slowly as he tried to work out the riddle. "And we know that you can timeslip—"

"And Caspian told us you're a thief," interrupted Madeleine, jumping to her own conclusion. "So you slipped into the future and stole it from Alfie?"

"*Was* a thief," said Ashford. "And no, I didn't steal it. I can't timeslip into the future, only the past, the late 1400s to be precise. Eighty-one years after the date my great-grandfather was born."

"If your great-grandfather was born in the 1400s, then you *must* have travelled into the future," said Robin. "How else could you be here?"

Amy felt the butler's forehead. "You're not making sense, Ash," she said. "Why don't you have a rest while we call Caspian."

"Caspian will be on his way. You can be sure of that," said Ashford, watching Alfie carefully. A spark of comprehension was flickering in Alfie's brain, shining a light on all of the unanswered questions about Ashford.

"It's me, isn't it?" he said quietly. "Your great-grandfather . . . is me. Your talisman is mine, only a later version. You inherited it from me?"

Ashford beamed at him. "Along with a few other gifts. I was the only one of your descendants to inherit the timeslip ability. Just as you can travel back nearly six hundred years to the lifetime you would have lived in the 1400s, I can travel that same distance back from my own birth, eighty-one years after yours."

"You're . . . from the future?" gaped Robin.

If Alfie wasn't already sitting down he would have fallen over.

Ashford nodded. "I am able to live here in this time period because Muninn and Bone have their own ways of manipulating time and sent me here to protect you." He looked down. "I haven't exactly done a great job of that so far."

"Hey, we're here, aren't we?" said Alfie. "And the elves would still be here if you hadn't had that idea about the talisman."

Amy, Robin and Madeleine were looking from Alfie to Ashford as though they had just found out the two of them were aliens.

"When was the last time you went back home –

back into the future?" Robin burst out. "Could you take us with you?"

Ashford was silent for a moment. "I can never go back. Mr Muninn made sure of that when he played with the threads of time to keep me here. It's part of my punishment, or so they thought."

Alfie hoped he'd never have to meet Mr Muninn. By the sound of him, he made even Caspian seem friendly by comparison.

Ashford twisted the talisman around his neck. "At first I thought it was an insult to be sent here to work for you, but I see now that it is the greatest thing that could have happened to me. I am proud to be of your family line, Alfie Bloom."

"All the amazing things you do around the castle – that's all with the magic you inherited?" asked Alfie. "The magic Orin hid inside me?"

"The magic was greatly watered down through the generations," said Ashford. "It is stronger in me than any of your other descendants, but it isn't close to what you hold." He shook his head. "I don't know how you do it – how you keep it from consuming you. I ignored the warnings you gave me when I was a child. I gave it far too much freedom and ended up serving out my punishment under Caspian's thumb."

"No," said Alfie. "You ended up at home. With family." He clasped Ashford's hand in what he felt was a manly shake.

The moment was broken by loud cawing as Caspian's ravens returned to the walls of Hexbridge Castle. The largest swooped straight down towards them, growing larger and changing in form until it was a man clothed in black.

Caspian Bone.

The solicitor's clawed feet turned to polished black shoes as they hit the ground mid stride. His huge wings folded and transformed into arms as he walked towards Alfie.

Caspian's head twitched quickly from side to side as his obsidian eyes took in the imprisoned elven Queen, the trees that had torn the castle entrance apart, and the ruins of the tower.

"You are unharmed?" he asked curtly.

"We're fine," said Alfie. "They tried to—"

"The crown?" said Caspian.

"Destroyed," replied Ashford, standing firm as Caspian marched over to stand toe to toe with him.

"You did not keep to the terms of our agreement," said the solicitor. "Not only did you travel beyond this village, you opened a portal to another realm and led *an army* straight to the child. You failed in your duty to protect him."

"That's unfair," said Alfie, stung at being called a child. He pointed at the Queen who was sitting quiet and still in the presence of Caspian. "If it wasn't for Ashford, Hexbridge would be in *her* realm and *we'd* all be slaves."

"If it wasn't for Ashford, Hexbridge wouldn't have needed saving," said Caspian without taking his eyes off the butler. "Your parole is over. You will return to our offices and we will discuss your punishment with Mr Muninn."

"He's not going anywhere," said Alfie. He wanted Ashford to say something, to fight back against Caspian, but he just stood there in silence.

"He feels guilty," whispered Robin. "He wants to be punished."

"Hey, look up there!" said Madeleine suddenly.

A strange black shape broke through the silvery moonlit clouds and hurtled down towards them. There was a loud whinny as the Muninn and Bone coach thundered down out of the sky to land beyond the castle walls. They heard twelve pairs of hooves hit the hillside one by one as six horses slowed to a canter.

"I knew it," shouted Amy, punching the air. "I

totally knew that thing could fly!"

"Quick, lower the drawbridge," said Madeleine, hopping from foot to foot. Alfie pulled out his key ring and pressed the remote control tag. The portcullis rattled upwards and the drawbridge clanked down to bridge the moat just in time for the steaming horses to clop across into the courtyard. Johannes, the driver, tipped his hat to Alfie as the coach rolled to a stop. The doors flew open and Alfie's dad, Granny, Aunt Grace and Uncle Herb leapt out and raced towards them.

No one could hold a conversation for several minutes with all the hugging and tears and a hundred questions all at once.

"Two days!" Aunt Grace kept crying. "Two days of not knowing what was happening in here."

"We couldn't break through the mist," said Alfie's dad, holding him tight around the shoulders. "We tried, but we kept forgetting what we were trying to do."

"And we couldn't get help," added Uncle Herb. "All the folks down in the village seemed to have forgotten there was ever a castle here. We were starting to find it difficult to remember too, but your dad finally managed to contact Caspian."

"I must have tied notes to the legs of ten

different ravens," said Alfie's dad. "One of them must have got the message to Caspian and he sent the coach for us. We've been at Muninn and Bone's offices since morning, waiting for the mist to fade."

"All of them brought your message, Mr Bloom," sighed Caspian. "Not that we needed it. They were most aggrieved at having notes tied to them like common homing pigeons. Simply telling them would have been enough."

Aunt Grace began to fuss over everyone again, but a strange silence fell as someone else stepped out of the coach.

"Emily," Ashford whispered under his breath.

"Ashford," Emily stood nervously by the coach, her long green dress flowing over the cobbles. "It's really you." She took a step towards him and then faltered, as though unsure whether to go to him. It was all the encouragement Ashford seemed to need. He ran towards her, swept her up into his arms, and buried his face in her hair.

"So, who'd like a nice cup of tea?" Aunt Grace said brightly, trying to distract everyone from the couple wrapped tightly in each other's arms.

"I'll give you a hand, love," said Uncle Herb gruffly. He followed her through the ruined doors of the castle, carrying a large picnic basket.

"I *knew* something was wrong when you wouldn't see me," said Emily. "But Caspian just said that at least one of us had come to our senses." She turned to the solicitor. "See, you're not always right. Just because *she* can't bear humans doesn't mean I can't choose who I want to be with." Caspian pretended not to hear as he walked away to inspect the damage to the castle.

"Who does she mean by *she*?" asked Granny.

"*Her*," said Madeleine, as Emily walked over to the Queen.

Artan realized everyone was looking at him. His eyes went dull and he let himself slip from the Queen's shoulders as if he was nothing more than a rug. The Queen stood up and brushed down her robes indignantly.

"That's her? The one behind all of this?" said Granny. "Who does she think she is? Sitting there wearing Alfie's rug like she's the Queen of Sheba!" She rolled up her sleeves and began to march towards her. Alfie's dad grabbed her quickly around the waist.

"Hold on, Mary. There's something going on here – better not get between them." Granny straightened her jumper then crossed her arms and watched the Queen like an eagle, as though daring her to try something. But the Queen only had eyes for Emily, staring down at her with a strange expression on her face. She began to speak in Elvish, but Emily shook her head.

"English," she said sharply. The Queen stiffened, but continued in English.

"Why do you wear this glamour? If we are to talk, take on your true form."

As Alfie watched, something seemed to shimmer around Emily, and suddenly she was taller. Her face mirrored the Queen's own beauty, but her features were softer and kinder.

"Happy now, Mum?" she said.

"Mum?" gasped Amy looking to Alfie. "Did you know?"

"Not a clue." Alfie's head was reeling. Emily Fortune, Caspian Bone's administrator, was the daughter of the Elven Queen? And she was in love with Ashford? So *she* was the other thing the Queen thought Ashford had stolen from her.

"Was it worth it?" sneered the Queen. "Helping a thief steal from your mother, your Queen? Was it worth being banished from your home? To work for a crow?" Caspian was still examining the damage to the castle, but Alfie saw him stiffen at her words.

"Banishment was the best thing to happen to me," said Emily. "You used the lens exactly as I knew you would. It should never have been in your hands. I *had* to call on Ashford's help to take it, for your own sake. You saw how Merioch turned your soldiers against you for its power. Its purpose now is far more noble."

"*Ashford*," spat the Queen, her eyes flickering to the butler. "You insult your entire race by consorting with this *human* thief. This unworthy—"

"ENOUGH!" said Emily, fire burning in her eyes as a shadow of the Queen's own temper appeared in her face. "I make *my own* choices." The shadow passed and her voice softened as she stepped back. "Caspian will pronounce the punishment for what you have done here."

Alfie jumped out of Caspian's path as he strode towards the Queen, her crow insult obviously still burning in his ears.

"As of today, the elven realm is in exile. There will be no trade with your race. All doorways, portals and paths between your realm and other lands will be sealed. For one hundred years."

Colour rose in the Queen's pale cheeks but she seemed to know better than to argue with Caspian. She nodded stiffly.

"Only chosen ambassadors will be able to visit your realm. Your army will be dispersed, and if there is even a thought of invading other lands. . ." He paused for dramatic effect. "The exile will be one thousand years." He pointed at the portal. "Now go."

The Queen turned, then paused in front of the shimmering portal.

"Why's she just standing there?" said Robin. "She got off lightly. I thought she'd be straight through."

"I'll say she got off lightly!" said Granny. "I'll help her through that thing with the end of my boot!"

"She's scared," said Alfie, surprised to find himself feeling sorry for her. "Her soldiers turned against her and her big plan failed. She probably doesn't know who to trust back home."

The Queen turned to Emily, her face no longer confident and cruel as she said in a wavering voice, "Come with me?"

Emily took her hand. "For a short while," she said gently. "I do have a job to get back to. That place would fall apart without me." She winked at Caspian who raised a single eyebrow in response.

"Don't go," said Ashford suddenly dashing forwards. "Not yet." He held something tightly clenched in one fist. "The reason I went back, after all that happened . . . well, it was to have something made. I thought I had gone undetected the first time. But when I went back to collect it, they followed me through."

"I don't understand," said Emily. "What was important enough for you to take that risk?"

"You," said Ashford. He knelt on the cobbles before her. Emily's hands flew to her mouth.

"No way!" said Amy, clutching Alfie's arm, Madeleine grabbed the other and bit her knuckles nervously.

"What?" asked Alfie, looking to Robin who shook his head in equal confusion.

"Shhhh!" hushed Granny. Even Alfie's dad was frozen to the spot.

"Emily Fortune," said Ashford, opening his hand to reveal a silvery elven ring glowing with white moonstones. "Will you marry me?"

Alfie didn't even hear her answer over Amy and Madeleine's shouts of delight, but he guessed Emily must have said yes as Ashford slipped the ring on to her finger and they kissed.

"Ugh, well there's no need for that," said

Madeleine, quickly looking away. Emily wiped a tear from her face as everyone rushed over to congratulate them. Even Caspian stiffly shook hands with them both.

Alfie's dad patted Ashford on the back. Alfie smiled at the two of them together and decided it might be just a bit too weird to let his dad know that Ashford was his great-great-grandson.

The Queen's lips were pressed together so hard they had turned white, but as Ashford and Emily looked to her she gave a nod so slight it was barely noticeable.

"Well, that's more approval than I ever expected from Mum," grinned Emily. "Goodbye for now, Ashford." She hugged him tightly. "I'll return as soon as things are settled back in the realm. And you..." she turned to Caspian, suddenly fierce again. "There will be no punishment for Ashford. Do you hear me? He was kidnapped, tortured and nearly killed. I think that's punishment enough, don't you?"

Caspian went even paler than his usual shade, something that Alfie wouldn't have thought possible. His jaw tightened as he said, "There is more to it than that. He broke our pact and led an army of elves to Alfie's door—"

"And saved us from them!" said Alfie, stepping in front of Ashford. "The crown was destroyed. It can never be used again." Amy, Madeleine and Robin rushed to flank him between the butler and the solicitor.

"You see?" said Emily. "Alfie has forgiven him, so there's no need to take this to Mr Muninn."

"Yeah, he's not going anywhere with you," said Amy, still completely un-awed by Caspian.

The solicitor looked to Alfie. "You are happy for me to leave him here with you, after all that he has done?"

Alfie tilted his head back to look up at Caspian, his jaw thrust out. "He's not going anywhere," he said firmly.

"Then Ashford shall remain here on parole," said Caspian crisply, as though it was his own idea. "His first duty will be to rebuild the tower and clear up the destruction he has wrought."

"That's a bit unfair," said Alfie. But Ashford was grinning.

"It will be done by morning," he agreed.

Emily and Ashford shared one last lingering look and then Emily took the Queen's hand. "Come on then, Mum," she said, leading her through the portal.

As the ripples in the portal died down Caspian uncorked a bottle of highly scented oil, removed a calligraphy brush from his pocket and flexed his fingers.

"Now, to seal this portal properly."

"Wait," said Alfie quickly. "I nearly forgot, there's one left!"

"I'll get him," said Ashford. The butler disappeared into the castle, returning swiftly with Loth the elf, still in his elven long-johns. Alfie, Amy and the twins grabbed his arms and legs. Together the five of them carried him to the portal and, after a few big swings to build up momentum, hurled him through.

Madeleine stuck her head through the portal. "And don't come back," her muffled voice yelled after him.

"If that is all?" said Caspian. "I will need full concentration to seal this portal properly. Please refrain from disturbing me during the ritual."

"Refrain from disturbing," Granny muttered under her breath, as Caspian dipped his brush in the oil. He began to paint symbols that soaked straight into the dry bark leaving a faint glow in the dark. "I'll disturb him right in the—"

"Mary!" said Alfie's dad quickly. "Come on

everyone. Grace and Herb must have finished making the tea by now."

16

Out of the Wreckage

Alfie saw Aunt Grace crying into Uncle Herb's shoulder as he entered the kitchen. She quickly wiped her tears and hugged them all one by one.

"Come on. Eat, eat," she said, finishing laying the kitchen table with the food she had brought. Alfie looked greedily at the feast of sweet and savoury scones, carrot cake, muffins, biscuits, chocolate sponge, sandwiches in home-made buns, and sausage rolls.

"She hasn't stopped baking since that mist blew up," said Uncle Herb. "It's a good job this ended when it did, or there'd be a world flour shortage."

"Hush," said Aunt Grace, shoving an angel

cake into his mouth so quickly he began to cough crumbs across the kitchen. "Now, Ashford, tell me all about this proposal!" Aunt Grace made each of them recount it in detail in case anyone missed anything out.

"Alfie, can we take a walk?" whispered his dad when Alfie had finally eaten his fill and Aunt Grace was listening to the fourth retelling of Ashford's proposal. Alfie suspected it was her way of avoiding talking about the unpleasantness of the last two days. He slipped out of the kitchen with his dad and headed outside.

Caspian had laid down his brush and was making a complicated series of hand gestures and chanting something under his breath. He paid them no attention as they crossed the courtyard to walk around the garden on the other side.

Alfie told his dad about everything that had happened as they walked.

"Oh, good job, Robin!" he said as Alfie told him about how they had used the iron-tipped arrows and iron bombs against the elves. Alfie carefully left out the scarier and stranger chunks of the story, such as being captured and held at arrow-point, disguising himself as an elf, and travelling back in time. Having his son held captive by elves behind a mist of forgetfulness was enough strangeness for his dad to deal with right now.

They sat down on a bench under the apple trees. "Alfie, I can't imagine what you all went through. I can only thank the stars that Ashford was here with you." Alfie didn't think it wise to reveal that the Ashford they had been shut in with had turned out to be an evil sprite. "I've been thinking ... I'd understand if you want to leave this place."

"What do you mean, leave?" asked Alfie.

"After all this – do you even feel safe here now? If you want to leave, to live somewhere a little more ... normal, then we can pack our bags and leave tomorrow." He looked up as dawn began to breach the castle walls, spilling a golden ray of light into the courtyard. "Well, today."

Alfie smiled. "Since when have we liked normal?" He hugged his dad. The elves had tried to take everything from him, but they had failed. Just as Murkle and Snitch had failed. His inheritance might draw trouble like a magnet, but with Amy, the twins, Ashford and Artan by his side, nothing was going to take it from him. "This is our home. It always will be." His dad hugged him back until a melodic trilling made them look up into the trees. Something shiny was hopping from branch to branch. There was a sudden crack and a shower of small twigs and buds, and it toppled on to Alfie's lap.

"Leonardo's bird!" exclaimed Alfie's dad as the silver sparrow hopped to its feet, chirped, and shook out its feathers. "What is it doing out here?"

"The Queen did something to it," said Alfie, surprised that the bird had escaped the vortex. It bounced from Alfie's knee and fluttered up to his dad's shoulder where it nuzzled his face, chirruping.

"It seems to have a spark of life in it now. I think it likes you."

"Amazing," whispered his dad as he stroked the bird's feathers gently with one finger. It threw back its head and began to whistle happily. "I think that's what we'll call it. Sparky."

"It is done," Caspian's voice cut crisply through the silence. Alfie and his dad hurried over to shake hands with the solicitor as he tucked the little jar and brush into his inner pocket. "The portal is secure. My sentinels will guard your walls, but you may sleep peacefully. Now, if you will excuse me, I have a temporary administrator to find in Ms Fortune's most inconvenient absence."

He climbed into the coach and Johannes turned the horses, talking them into a gallop across the drawbridge, down the hillside and then up into the air.

"One day I need to ask him exactly how that works," said Alfie's dad as the coach disappeared into the clouds.

"I don't think you'll get an answer."

"Me neither."

Ashford was waiting for them by the wreckage of the front door.

"They're all off to bed for a few hours' sleep," he told them. "There are enough rooms made up for everyone. I'll secure the castle before retiring myself."

"Just shut the drawbridge," yawned Alfie's dad. "There's nothing we can do about this door right now."

"You'd be surprised at what I can do when I put my mind to it," said Ashford.

"I can believe that."

"Dad, I'll go up in a few minutes," said Alfie as his dad joined the others traipsing wearily up the stairs, Sparky still happily bobbing up and down on his shoulder. Alfie had seen something in Ashford's face that indicated he wanted to talk to him. "I'm just going to get some milk."

"OK. But don't be long. See you this afternoon."

Once they were alone, Ashford waved his hand at the door and tower. "I thought you could help me with this little problem. And at the same time, we can take care of this change magic that's bothering you. That is, if you're *sure* you want to be rid of it?"

"One-hundred-per-cent positive!" said Alfie immediately. It wasn't just its unpredictability and the fact that it came from Murkle and Snitch that bothered him, it was the way it seemed it have a mind of its own, just like the ancient magic. After all the books and comics he had read, he had never imagined that possessing magic would be a bad thing. "How do we do this?"

"I could show you how to use it yourself," said Ashford. "Teach you how to burn up the change magic with the creation magic Orin gave you and create something physical with it. I *could* do that, but your magic grows hungrier the more it is fed; I fear what it would do to your mind."

"I don't want to use it," said Alfie firmly. "Is there another way?"

Ashford nodded.

"I will let the magic I inherited from you feed on it. It is much less powerful than yours, but I can use it to recreate what has been destroyed."

"What do I need to do?" asked Alfie.

"Just this." Ashford held out his left palm. Alfie placed his right palm against it. The butler opened his top button to reveal his own talisman on his chest. "Ready?" he asked. Alfie nodded. Almost immediately he felt something flowing from his chest, down his left arm and through his hand. The change magic was leaving him, being absorbed by Ashford's creation magic – the very magic that he had inherited from Alfie. So *this* was why Orin had said the butler was the only one who could help!

The lens in the talisman on Ashford's chest started to glow as the magic flowed faster and faster down Alfie's arm. He felt a little queasy and his legs began to wobble until Ashford finally removed his hand, the talisman on his chest now glowing bright white.

"Sorry, Alfie," he said. "I'd have warned you, but I had to take it quickly, before Orin's magic realized I was stealing from it. Fortunately it is weaker and tamer inside me, but I still allowed it too much freedom for many years. It started to corrupt me. Never underestimate it. Now, are you ready to see how I really get things done?"

Alfie watched as Ashford threw his arms wide and looked up at the castle. A bright white beam shone out of the talisman and up to the empty space the top of the tower used to inhabit. In the beam, bricks started to form, pouring out of the light and swirling around as though in a cyclone. As they swirled, the bricks started to lay themselves one by one on the wall. Alfie watched the strange sight in silent awe. As the final bricks were laid, a new beacon appeared at the very top. The tower was complete again.

"Well, did I get it right?"

"It's as good as new!" said Alfie incredulously.

"Next time you see Orin, you must remember to tell him not to store anything important on the upper floors," said Ashford.

"I have a feeling I will," grinned Alfie. "Is there enough energy left to fix the doors?"

"Not quite," said Ashford. "But those trees should do the job." He placed his right hand on one of the trees that had grown from the castle door. "Stand back. They're holding up loose brickwork."

Alfie stepped back and watched as, under the butler's touch, the tree began to shrink back, leaves and trunk shrivelling. Bricks crashed loudly to the ground as the branches that supported them curled up, but everyone in the castle was in too deep a sleep to hear or care. At last the tree turned grey before finally dissolving into dust before Alfie's eyes.

"You can see why this magic had to be kept out of the wrong hands," said Ashford as he repeated the process on the other tree. "Something that feeds on energy and life to create anything you desire cannot be allowed to go free."

As the second tree crumbled to dust, Ashford let the magic flow through the talisman again, recreating the doors and wall seemingly out of thin air. Finally the castle was just as it had been before the invasion.

"Doesn't it drive you mad to use it?" asked Alfie, remembering the whisperings in his head whenever the magic tried to force its way out.

"Something as big as this makes it itch at the back of my skull," said Ashford. "I usually use thefires in the castle to draw energy for things like the stage for your play last year, and the Christmas tree."

"I was wondering how you managed to get that huge thing up the hill," grinned Alfie.

"Just remember, don't try to use it yourself," said Ashford seriously. "I have trained with the magic for years. Now, bed!"

Alfie left Ashford to lock the newly made doors as he climbed the stairs to his room. It was still almost too much to believe that his own great-grandson was working as his magical butler.

It seemed like months since he had last slept in his bed. His room was still upside down after the elves' search for the lens, but he didn't care. Throwing himself face first into his soft pillows he sank gratefully into sleep.

"Al. *Al!* WAKE UP, AL!"

Alfie tore himself from sleep as a bright light shone through his eyelids. Amy had flung his curtains wide.

"Wha. . .?" he asked, rubbing his eyes.

"I just spoke to Gran," she laughed as she bounced on to the end of the bed. "She didn't half tell me off for not calling for two days, but she's well on the mend."

"That's great," said Alfie, sitting up and furtively wiping the drool from his cheek.

"She said that the illness made her think things over and she wants a change of scenery. So guess what? You'll *never* guess!"

"So just tell me then," said Alfie, exasperated by this energetic wake-up call.

Amy did a little spin of joy and threw her arms wide. "We're moving to Hexbridge!"

Alfie jumped out of bed, staggering as he

realized one leg was still asleep. He hopped over to Amy through pins and needles for a high five, fist bump and hug in quick succession.

"I'm going to tell Maddie and Robin," she yelled. "Oh man, school is going to be so much fun! By the way, one of Caspian's ravens dropped this off for you. It was pecking at the window for ages but gave up and dropped it down to me in the courtyard." She threw him a yellowed envelope then dashed out of the room. "Later, Al!"

Alfie sat down and rubbed life back into his leg. He couldn't believe the news. His best mate was moving to Hexbridge. The day couldn't really get much better.

He looked at the envelope in his hands. Written on the front in Orin's slanting script was today's date. Orin must have left the letter with Caspian to be delivered on this particular day. He opened it to see a blank page. Remembering the last letter he had received from Orin, he put the talisman to his eye like a monocle and read the now visible text through its lens.

Dear Alfie,
    I asked for this letter to be delivered to you after the situation with the elves resolved itself, as I had no doubt it would.

Alfie was a little surprised at how easily Orin shrugged off what could have been a huge disaster, but the druid seemed to have unusual ways of finding things out. He continued to read...

You have almost mastered the use of your timeslip ability and encountered threats I could not foresee. Therefore I have decided to begin your training early, six months before the traditional age of thirteen.

It is your choice, but if you are willing, please send word to Caspian through his ravens. He has his ways of communicating through time. The castle is yours, whatever you decide, but I hope to train you in our ways, for your protection and that of your loved ones and also to carry our sacred knowledge and traditions into your world, which must be suffering for lack of the old knowledge.

On receipt of your answer I will either accept your decision, or begin to prepare your first lesson.

Your friend, always,
Orin Hopcraft.

Alfie read the letter again and then placed it into one of the secret compartments in his bed. His inheritance had brought great danger twice now, and he knew it wouldn't be the last time. He had accepted the castle, and now it was time to conquer the magic that came with it.

A raven was waiting on the window sill. Alfie opened the window and met the bird's black eyes.

"Yes," he said.

The raven bobbed its head, leapt from the sill and soared away into the sky. Alfie watched as it disappeared into the clouds, dreaming of what Orin would teach him.